THE COST OF LOVING YOU 3

The Finale

REIGN LEE

SYNOPSIS

Coming out of a coma, the life that Shanell knew with Jaylen no longer existed. The news of him having amnesia and him not recognizing her had broken her to her core. It also put her in a more vulnerable state, giving whoever was trying to hurt her a better chance at succeeding. With her now finding out that she will be a mother, Shanell decides to hold on to this secret, in hopes that the man she loves will remember her and what they once meant to each other. But will it be before she starts to show? Will her secret be exposed? Will she even make it through the pregnancy to tell Jaylen he's going to be a father, when he has no idea who she is? A decision must be made before it's all too late.

Figuring out who he is and trying to adjust, Jaylen feels like he's been granted a new start. Everyone has a clean slate, even

Nikki. Being the only one that he remembers, he makes it a point to find out more about her. Hearing that they have a baby on the way, Jaylen feels obligated, now more than ever, to be by her side. As he settles into his celebrity, he realizes a whole lot of other women want him by their side too. Will he give in to all this temptation, making Shanell an afterthought? Or will his memory finally return to him, making him realize there's no place like home? See how this whole ordeal plays out in *The Cost of Loving You Finale*, and find out if this is really the end.

Chapter One

INVITING MORE TROUBLE

 *ay*

"You said they?"

"Paging Dr. Mitchell! Paging Dr. Mitchell!"

"I'm sorry. Can you excuse me for a second?" Just like that, the doctor left out. Kelli came to his defense since she noticed I was still looking puzzled with no answer given. "The doctor just meant with her care... They're doing very well with her care."

"Thanks for explaining that to me. I thought... never mind. I think I'mma... uh... I'mma head out." Her sudden movement had me feeling uneasy.

"Sure!"

As I walked out the room, I was curious about the story behind someone tryna hurt her. I asked Spence to explain the situation as we walked to the elevators.

"This is new information to all of us, man."

I could tell he was holding back. It was all in his eyes and his mannerisms. Just didn't seem like his usual M.O. when I would ask him things. I didn't know if it was because they still didn't wanna overwhelm me, or if it was something worse. I was gonna get to the bottom of it eventually. Once we got off the elevators, some chick called my name.

"Jay!"

From the looks on everyone's faces, no one was thrilled to see her, especially Momma.

"Nikki, sweetheart, Jay really has to go," Momma declared as this Nikki chick closed in on us.

"Please, Ms. Murphy, I'll only need a moment." Then her name clicked. That was Nikki, the one name I remembered. Damn! She was gorgeous too. She anxiously tried to get near me, but Spence held her back. Her almond shaped eyes burned into me as she spoke with desperation. "Jay, since you refused to believe me before, please just look at this," she begged, tryna hand me what she had.

I looked at Momma, who stared at Nikki, mad as hell. She angrily snatched it from her, which shocked the shit out of me. I'd never seen her react that way toward someone since I'd been home. Something definitely was up, which only heightened my need to know.

"What she talkin' 'bout?" Momma stared at me, not

wanting to answer. It was like she was tryna protect me from whatever this was, but fuck that! I needed to know, and I wanted to know now! "Lemme see that."

Reluctantly, she put it in my hand. Instantly, my heart started beating rapidly, causing a ringing sound in my ears as I tried to process what this shit was. Momma could see I was having a hard time grasping it and put her hands on my shoulders, but in that moment, I didn't wanna be touched and aggressively shrugged them off me.

"What the fuck is this?"

"The prenatal appointment. I thought since you didn't believe me, you could come and see for yourself." I looked around at everybody that was standing there. "What she talking 'bout?"

Nikki didn't give anybody a chance to say anything.

"Jay, I already told you this is your baby I'm carrying. If you don't believe I'm pregnant, come to the appointment."

"You s'pose to be pregnant by me?"

Nikki pulled her head back and raised her eyebrows in confusion.

"Ms. Murphy, is he okay?"

"You know, Nikki, he's not fully recovered from his own accident, so it would've been nice if you could've taken that into consideration before you thought about yourself."

Nikki held her mouth open like she just had a revelation about something.

"I wasn't even thinking... I'm sorry... I heard he was here

and... you're right, but I didn't want to miss this chance to see him."

"It's funny that I ran into you though." I gave her back the appointment slip. "I wanted to know who you were, but you're telling me I'm the father of your baby?" She had this look on her face like she was blown away.

"Jay, what do you mean you wanted to know who I was—"

Momma locked her arm in mine.

"Okay, Jay, let's not discuss this in here right now. Nikki, Jay will call you."

"Nah, I don't wanna talk about this on no phone. Do you know where I live?"

She scrunched up her face like she was so confused as her eyes strolled over everyone before coming back to me.

"No. I've never been to your place."

"Have I ever been to yours?"

"Yeah! Jay, what's going on?"

"We'll have someone come get you so we can talk. What time you get off?"

"At three o'clock pm."

"Someone will be at your place around five. Is that cool?"

"Y-Yeah... sure."

"Alright! I'll see you later."

Once Nikki walked off, Momma continued to express her disapproval of Nikki.

Janine

Everyone knew that Jay didn't remember Nikki and all the

things that she'd done, but no one was pleased with him wanting her to come to his house.

"Jay, I know you don't have your memory back yet, but I don't think it's a good idea for you to invite Nikki over."

"Why not? Is she really s'pose to be pregnant by me?"

We started walking as we talked.

"We don't really know that for sure. That's why—"

"It's a chance though, right?"

"You were with her, so yes, it is a chance unfortunately, but Jay, we—"

His footsteps stopped as he showed his emotions.

"Momma, why are you so upset by this? I could be a father. Why you not happy for me?"

"Jay, it's a lot you don't remember where Nikki is concerned. I wouldn't get too attached to the idea of that baby."

"What you mean?"

"Baby, let's finish this discussion at home." As soon as we walked in the house, Jay was asking me to explain what I meant. We walked and had a seat in the family room to talk. He sat and gave me his undivided attention. "Jay, listen to me. Nikki has caused a lot of problems for you and Shanell in the past and still to this day. Even down to this pregnancy. She's just a pretty face to you right now, but baby, she has some serious issues."

"That may be true, and I may not remember everything that went down with me and her, but if she's carrying my baby, I owe it to my child to be there for its mother."

I rested the top of my hand over his. I really needed him to understand.

"Jay, we don't even know if this baby is really yours yet."

"You said there's a chance it's mine, right?" I squeezed his hand a little tighter as I spoke. It hurt me to see him clueless as to the type of woman that Nikki was.

"Okay, but we won't know that for sure until we can get a DNA test done, which likely won't take place until after the baby is born."

"All I wanna do is talk to her, so can you get off my back?" he barked. My head and my hand snapped back at his remark. I knew he wasn't in his right mind to raise his voice and fix his lips to say that shit to me, but I surely had all my wits and wasn't about to hesitate to let him know it. He didn't know, but he was going to find out just how much of a mom I was about to be.

"You listen here, negro!" I pointed my finger directly in his face. His eyes grew wide the moment he saw it and heard my tone. "You may not remember me as your mother, but damnit you will respect me, regardless. I care about you and your sister like you wouldn't believe, so if you feel like I'm on your back on this, I have to be, and I won't apologize for it. You, on the other hand, owe me one, now!"

"I'm sorry. I didn't mean to speak to you that way." He stood up. "I just want to do the right thing. I may even go with her to this doctor's appointment. I just needa know what's goin' on for myself."

"That's understandable, Jay, but even if she told you, you

still wouldn't know what's really going on. I do, baby, and I'm only trying to tell you because you don't realize the things that I already know to be true right now. Do you really need for her to come here to find out whatever it is you feel you need to know? She shouldn't be coming up in your home, Jaylen. How do you think Shanell would feel about that if she knew?"

"I can't worry about that right now. I need some answers from her, and talking on the phone is not how I wanna handle it." I stood back up, appalled.

"Nikki is dangerous, Jay. Someone has already tried to hurt Shanell, and you wanna welcome Nikki into your home? You're inviting more trouble."

"I don't see it that way. It's only a conversation."

"You won't see it that way because you don't know all the facts!"

"Stop telling me what I don't know! That's already apparent. I can't change none of that, Momma. I'm doing this *my way*, okay?" I took both of Jay's hands in mine.

"Baby, sit down with me please." We sat down together, and I tried once more to speak to him in a calmer manner. "Baby, I know you don't remember this, but we talk about everything. You knew you could always come to me because no matter what it was, I would never turn my back on you... or even judge you, but more importantly, I'm always honest with you. I want nothing but the best for you, Jay, and will always have your best interest at heart. I'm saying what I'm saying to you because I love you, and right now, with this situation, you don't have all the facts and clear judgement, whether you want to hear it or not. But you're an adult, and no matter how much I disagree with your decisions sometimes, I can't make you do anything. If you do nothing else, Jaylen,

don't have her all over this house, and when you do talk to her, tell her you want a DNA test. That's all I ask, before you get caught up in a child's life that's not even yours."

"I can appreciate ya words, and I'll consider what you saying."

Nikki

Five o'clock came around, and I was picked up and on my way to Jay's house. My heart was racing so fast as my eyes roamed through the neighborhoods, watching as the homes in certain areas became bigger and bigger. I didn't know what was going on with Jay, but whatever this change was, I was so grateful for it. Everyone was there when I arrived. Politely, I spoke and then followed behind Jay as he led the way into a massive family, sitting, or even a showroom. Whatever it was, it was beautiful.

"Jay, this place is amazing!" All I could do was smile as I imagined what it would be like to wake up to this every day. Imagining the pictures I noticed of him and Shanell hanging around the house being the two of us instead. But what I envisioned the most was him climbing in the bed by my side each night. Oh, how delicious and romantic each one would be.

"Nikki."

"Huh!" I answered, startled.

"You can have a seat."

"Oh, I'm sorry. I was somewhere else for a minute." I still was in awe from what I had seen thus far. This room had floor to ceiling windows on one wall that let in so much light. Along with the fact that the furniture in it was white with black accessories. It was

decorated so elegantly and dripped of money. I sat down first, then he sat beside me on the couch. "Jay, this house is a dream. I love it!"

"Thanks!"

It was like being on top of the world in his presence. I never wanted to come down.

"I can't even believe you invited me over to talk."

"Why you say that?" When he smiled at me, it just fucked my whole world up. It was so mesmerizing and genuine.

"Come on, Jay, don't act like you usually give me the time of day, which I can understand why you didn't anymore. I have, er um, done some wild and crazy things," I not so eagerly admitted. "But it was all because—" I sincerely looked him in the eyes "—I love you."

He raised his thick eyebrows like what I said was in a foreign language.

"You love me?" he repeated.

"I know doing the things that I've done may not seem like love, but honestly, it was all out of love for you."

"So when did we break up?"

I studied his face.

"Jay, something is different with you... what is it?" I questioned as I touched his hand. He looked at me at first as if it was going to be a problem, but then he let my hand stay there and put his other one on top of mine.

"Look, to be honest with you, I don't even know who you are. When I fell, they told me I lost my memory. I'm just tryna figure things out."

I laid my hand flat on my chest.

"You don't remember me?"

"I'm sorry... but I don't."

I sighed. I didn't know what to make out of this at all.

"Wow... I didn't know, but now things make sense."

"So what's our story? How'd we come to possibly have a baby together?"

Like I'm going to ruin this by telling the truth.

"Well uh... this particular time, I had won a contest to have dinner with you. We ate and had a few drinks. One thing led to another, and needless to say, I got pregnant."

"So... we had drunk sex?" he casually asked.

"Hahaha! No, boy! We might've been a little tipsy, but we knew what we were doing."

"Was I engaged when this happened?"

"No, this happened before that, but Jay, one thing you

should know about us is that I was your first love. You and I go way back."

"So why'd we break up?"

I took my focus off him, crossed my hands in my lap, and sadly stared at the expensive flooring before responding.

"You left me for Shanell."

"And you was still letting me hit it?"

That made me laugh. I eyed him adoringly.

"As I said before, I love you. You can't resist me, and I surely can't resist you. We still have this connection to each other that's hard to break. Now it's a bond." I took Jay's hand and placed it on my belly. "The result of our love is right here."

He held it there for a second. The warmth of it seeped right through me, giving me tingles. Then he removed it, interrupting the current that had me electrified.

"So why I'm marrying Shanell and not you?"

"Why are you getting married at all is the question. I don't think you really want to."

"I definitely can't be ready if I'm cheating and shit."

"Well, that's something you still have control over."

"Yeah, it's a lot to think about, but about this baby. Would you be willing to take a DNA test?"

"Of course."

"Alright."

Janine

I decided to go peek in on Jay and Nikki. She stayed over for a good while. In doing so, I saw the two of them laughing and talking to each other like they were best friends. That gave me an idea. I made a phone call.

"Hello, Lyric."

Her voice sounded all groggy. I had completely forgot about the time difference.

"Hey, Mom... how are you?"

"I'm good. I'm so sorry to wake you, sweetheart. I really do apologize."

"No... it's okay. What's going on?"

"Listen, I don't know if you heard anything about Jay—"

"No! Why? Please don't tell me something's wrong again."

I heard all the sleepiness disappear after I said that.

"I don't want to alarm you, but he actually fell and hit his head and is now suffering from amnesia."

"No, Mom, please don't tell me that."

"Yeah, I know. He's home now, trying to get used to everyone and his life, but I was wondering if you were able to come here and see him again?"

I bit the corner of my lip as I waited for her response. I hated to ask her to come here for this, but I felt it was necessary.

"I'm there. I had no idea something happened to my Jay bear."

"I'm sorry I didn't get in touch with you sooner... It's been so much going on, but I'm hoping it will help his memory if he saw more faces."

"I will definitely be there to see him."

"Okay, great! Anything you need to get here, let me know."

"I will."

I hung up the phone with Lyric, hoping that him seeing her would bring his memory back. I didn't like what I was seeing with him and Nikki, and if things didn't jog his memory when she came, Shanell waking up was my only hope.

Sheila

Shanell had been in a coma for a total of two months now. When she had her ultrasound done, to their surprise, they noticed two babies. I got more excited. They were progressing along okay from what they could see. Their heart-beats were nice and strong, which was a really good sign. I was speechless about the thought of twins. She was now twelve weeks pregnant. Shanell was definitely high risk. They were concerned about her health deteriorating the longer she stayed in this state, and the babies surviving. It was hard for me to be completely happy because my baby was still in this vegetative state. I was really starting to get depressed and letting the stress take effect.

"Auntie, why don't you go to the condo and get some rest? I promise if anything changes with Shanell, I'll call you."

"Nevaeh, I'm afraid to leave her side. She has so much

going on with her right now. I feel like I need to be here to make sure she knows that I'm here."

"I know, Auntie, but you need to take care of yourself too. How can you be any good to Shanell if you're no good to yourself?"

"How'd you get so wise?"

"It runs in the family."

"I guess I will go to the condo and try to get a little sleep, but if anything changes... *anything*, please let me know, Nevaeh."

"I promise you I will."

I drove over to the condo and got some much-needed rest. I came back feeling refreshed and mentally prepared to deal with my daughter's situation again. Nevaeh and I were talking when suddenly Shanell opened her eyes. Nevaeh noticed it first and told me to look.

"Shanell! When I saw her face, her eyes were open. I got out of that chair so fast and walked beside the bed. Overwhelmed by it all, I was shaking. "Sweetheart! It's me! Mommy." The tears immediately began to fall. I had been praying for this day and was so happy it was finally here. "Hey."

"Auntie, do you want me to go get the nurse?"

"Yes, Nevaeh, if you don't mind." I gushed as my trembling hands cleared my eyes.

Nevaeh

I walked out of the room, and Mrs. Mable was there at the desk. I really didn't want to talk to her, but Kelli wasn't there.

"Shanell has her eyes open."

"Is she keeping them open like she's alert, or she still looks like she's daydreaming?"

"I'm not a nurse. That's why I came out here to get you. All I know is that her eyes are open, and they weren't before."

She folded her arms and stared at me like there was a problem.

"I'll be in there after I call her doctor."

I rolled my eyes at her and went back in the room.

"Oh my gosh! I can't stand that lady."

Sheila

"You're always fussing about Mrs. Mable. Leave that lady alone. Kelli wasn't out there?"

"No. I wish she would've been though."

Mrs. Mable came in the room along with Shanell's doctor. He checked her eyes to see if they were staying open because she was fully alert or just holding them open. He shined a light in them and checked her pupils. He also took a tissue and made it real pointy on the tip and brushed it over the top of her eyes to check her sensory reflexes. He moved her head side to side to see if her eyes would lag and then catch up or if they stayed focused.

Next, he checked her mouth to see how her gag reflexes were and her ability to cough. So far, Shanell was responding as she should. He checked her reflexes to see what her response would be. She did move her arms and legs as he tapped them. Then he dragged the scalpel on the bottom of each foot to see if she would react to that, and she did.

He started talking to Shanell and explaining to her what had been going on with her for the past two months, excluding her first month of the possible unknown pregnancy. He didn't tell her about it since he knew I wanted to. He asked her if she knew who I was, and she shook her head yes with a smile. That was a good sign and just warmed my heart. They still had more tests to do on her to see how well her brain was functioning, but the fact that she remembered and was responding well to the exercises were all good signs.

He gave Nevaeh and me some time alone with her and left the room. Shanell was coherent, but she wasn't saying anything. I basically was doing all the talking as Shanell appeared to be listening. She was starting to look sleepy.

"Baby, do you want to close your eyes and get some more rest?" She nodded her head yes. I kissed her and watched her as she fell back to sleep. That's when Nevaeh and I decided to go to the condo to do the same thing since now I could actually rest with less worry and come back the next day less burdened.

When we returned in the morning, Shanell looked more alert. She was watching TV when we walked in. I gave her the biggest hug, then Nevaeh did the same.

"Oh, sweetheart, it's so good to have you back with us again."

"I still don't..." She cleared her throat. "I still don't understand what happened."

I stroked her hair as I leaned on the bed beside her.

"And I'll explain all of that to you, but let's not concentrate on that right now okay? How are you feeling today?"

"My stomach feels queasy, and my body feels stiff." Suddenly, she touched her face repeatedly. "Is my surgery done? I don't feel my scar like before."

I noticed this revelation was getting her all worked up.

"Sweetheart, calm down please. You did get it done. They're just keeping it concealed, but the mark itself is gone."

Then Shanell looked at Nevaeh sitting there quietly the whole time.

"I owe you big time, don't I?" Everyone laughed, although I didn't get the joke.

"We'll call it even since you're finally awake."

"Nevaeh, I'm gonna see if I can get in touch with her father again. I'll be right back."

"Okay, Auntie."

*S*hanell

"I'm sorry, Nevaeh. Was Marcus mad?"

"Marcus! Jay is the one you need to be asking about."

"Jay was here to see me, wasn't he? I heard him."

The thought of him made me smile.

"Yes, he came to see you."

"So, he knows?"

"Yes, Shanell, he knows. Do you remember what the doctor explained to you?"

"Wait a minute. I'm just realizing I'm not in the other office. I'm in the hospital?"

"Yes. Shanell that's what the doctor was explaining to you. You have been in a
coma."

I sat myself up more.

"I remember him saying that... I don't know... It didn't register, I guess. What happened?"

"Oh no! I'm not telling you. Auntie will explain it."

"The last thing I remember was going under before my surgery."

"Yeah, well, it's a lot that's happened since then, but I'll let Auntie Sheila explain all that."

"Nevaeh, hurry... Give me that basin. I gotta throw up!" Nevaeh grabbed it and held it for me. I almost made Nevaeh sick as I vomited, so she looked away. My mother came back in the room with Kelli, and at this point, I was dry heaving.

"Oh my gosh! Baby, are you okay?"

Nevaeh gave me some tissues to wipe my mouth.

"Hi, Shanell. I'm Kelli, one of your nurses. Is your stomach bothering you?"

"It's a little unsettling."

"Okay. Well, that's just normal, so you can expect that to happen, okay."

"Ugh! I hope it doesn't happen anymore. I hate throwing up."

Kelli looked at my mom suspiciously as she stood beside Nevaeh. I found that odd but brushed it off.

"Well, Shanell, I'm so happy to see that you're up, girl. You've been very popular on this floor. I couldn't wait to meet this person that is so loved and held in such high regard."

"Thank you, Kelli."

"Shanell, Kelli has taken real good care of you since you've been in here... Mrs. Mable too," my mom added.

"If that's coming from her, Kelli, then I definitely believe it."

"Aw... I'm just doing my job."

"No really, Kelli. You have been great with keeping me informed and staying positive when you saw I was having a hard time. I really am grateful to you for that."

"I'm glad I could do that for you, Mrs. Weiss, and thank you."

"Your cousin has been here too, Shanell, every step of the way. She even had surgery and still came back to be with you and I."

"Aw... she knows I love her. What happened for you to need surgery?"

"Had an accident at my job. Hurt my back."

Kellie took the basin to empty it out.

"Yeah, I owe you. As soon as I get out of here, we're gonna go hang out and get some drinks."

My mom and Nevaeh switched places and she sat down beside me.

"Well, Shanell, you might wanna put that off for a while."

"Where is Jay? Has anyone called him?"

"I did call him when I spoke to your dad. I left him a message. Which reminds me..." She kissed my cheek. "Your dad wanted me to do that. He told me to tell you that he loves you and will come see you as soon as he gets back."

"Okay, so why do we have to wait to go out?"

"Shanell, before you decided to have this surgery done,

was there anything that you might've wanted to share with me?"

"Mom, I know I didn't tell you about the surgery but—"

"I know, but I'm not talking about that. Was there anything else that you can think of that was new in your life that you wanted to share?"

I didn't know where her line of questioning was leading, but I was starting to get irritated.

"No. Mom, what's going on?"

"Well it looks like you're going to be a mom too, baby."

"A mom to who?"

"We don't know yet until you have the babies." I was stunned. "A baby? I'm pregnant?"

"Yes, sweetheart, you are." I sighed heavily as I looked toward the ceiling.

"This has got to be a mistake. Me and Jay are always cautious... at least I thought we were."

"Well, Shanell, you know birth control is not a hundred percent effective."

Out of nowhere, I started crying.

"But this can't be. We're not ready, and we haven't even got married yet."

My mom got up and wrapped her arms around me.

"Baby, it's going to be okay. You can still get married."

"And ready or not, cousin, you and Jay are gonna be parents."

I shook my head at the thought of all this.

"I don't believe it."

"Sweetheart, the doctor has already performed an ultrasound. I was there. I saw the babies." I got out from under my mother's embrace.

"Babies?"

"You're having twins."

"No! This can't be happening!" My eyes filled with tears more and more. This was not good news at all. Nevaeh gave me another tissue, and my mom moved closer to try to comfort me.

"Sweetheart, it's gonna be okay."

"No, it isn't! Does Jay know?"

"No. I haven't had a chance to say anything to him yet, and no one else has yet either, because I wanted to be the one to tell him. I just haven't run into him yet."

"I haven't said anything either, Shanell."

I wiped my eyes.

"I can only imagine how he's gonna feel about this. We're not ready."

"Sweetie, I never expected your reaction to be like this. I thought you would've been happy about it."

"I just feel so unprepared, and then to be having more than one. I'm not ready to be a mother yet. It's so much more I wanna do... that me and Jay wanna do."

"Cousin, you might not be able to do things like you used to, because you'll have little ones to consider, but you guys will still be able to do stuff. Your life's not over; it's only being enhanced. You're probably just emotional right now because of everything. I don't think you really mean what you're saying."

"I think Nevaeh's right. You've had a lot to digest today... probably more than what you should've."

"Can one of you call Jay again? I really wanna see him."

"I'll call him, Auntie."

"No, let me do it, Nevaeh. I need to call his mom anyway."

Sheila

I left the room to call Janine since I hadn't talked to her and to see if Jay told her Shanell woke up.

"Hey, Janine, it's Sheila."

"Sheila! It's good to hear from you. How you doing? Is everything okay with Shanell?"

"I'm doing wonderful, and yes, everything is fine with Shanell. She finally opened her eyes."

"Shanell's up?"

"Yes. Just came out of it yesterday, but she's more alert today."

"Oh, Sheila! I'm so happy to hear that. I'm going to have to come see her."

"I guess Jay hasn't had a chance to tell you then. I left him a message."

"Well, Jay can't even check his messages yet. I didn't tell you this because you were dealing with Shanell, but my baby is suffering with amnesia from his fall."

"What? Janine, I had no idea."

"I know, and the only reason why I didn't say anything was because you already had a lot you were dealing with."

"Oh no! Janine, you still could've told me that. Jay is like a son to me. Wow... I didn't know it was that serious."

"I know."

"Shanell wants to see him."

"Well, he's been there to visit her already, so he's aware of their history a little bit."

"I still can't believe he's suffering from amnesia."

"Me either. This is so hard to deal with. He doesn't even remember me."

"Janine, I can't even imagine what you're going through. I'm really sorry to hear that. You know I'm here if you need to talk or anything."

"I appreciate that, lady. I'll let Jay know Shanell's up, and we'll be by there to come see her."

"Okay. I'll see you when you get here then."

Shanell

Ms. Murphy and Jay arrived at the hospital. I was so happy to see them when they walked in.

"Hey, baby," she said as we hugged. "I'm so glad to see that beautiful face of yours sitting here with your eyes open." Ms. Murphy started casing the room. "Where's your mom?"

"She left for a minute to take Nevaeh back to the condo since her back was starting to bother her."

I was surprised that Jay didn't hug me first or even show any emotions like his mom did when he came in the room.

After his mom moved away, Jay gave me a hug, and instead of going for my lips, he went to kiss my cheek. I noticed right away too that his embrace didn't last very long, and it felt cold. His mom must've seen my reaction as Jay pulled away from me and immediately started talking.

"You gave us a scare, missy."

"So I've been hearing."

Jay joined in. "How you feeling?"

"I've been feeling a little nauseous since I've been up, but they said that's normal. Other than that, not too bad."

"Are they giving you anything for it?" his mom asked.

"They haven't yet." Jay suddenly had a look of concern on his face.

"You still feeling that way?"

"No, I'm okay right now. It seems to come and go." I patted the spot beside me.

"Baby, come over here by me."

He looked at his mom first before he had a seat. I lovingly looked him in the eyes as I locked my fingers with his. "I heard you talking to me, babe. You don't know how bad I wanted to touch you."

His eyes lit up as he smiled back.

"You could hear what I was saying to you?"

"I remember hearing your voice and it making me smile on the inside. I can't remember exactly what you were saying, but I knew you were here."

"Yeah, I was here."

"So how has the tour been?"

"From what I hear, we was killing it. It was a success."

"So, a lot of good press and feedback?"

"You could say that."

I sensed something was wrong with Jay. Then I thought he must really be mad at me. He hadn't really embraced me and had yet to show me how happy he was to see me awake. There was certainly a disconnect.

"So, Shanell," his mom said, breaking my thoughts. "I see the surgery besides the fact that it caused you to be in coma went very well. Your face looks good."

My hand automatically went to the spot.

"It does? Thanks! I haven't even seen it yet."

"Here, I have a mirror in my bag." She took it out and handed it to me. When I looked at myself, I was amazed at what I saw. Even though my hair was a mess, I had bags for days under my eyes, and my skin looked pale as a ghost, my face was now scarless, and I looked like the me I knew again.

"Wow, I... you're right. It really is covered up. It's really me again."

Jay started asking me questions finally about the surgery.

"Why you feel like you had to do that in the first place? You didn't think you were still beautiful?"

I could hear it in his voice that he was mad with me.

"I wanted to surprise you, and no. Part of me didn't feel beautiful anymore."

"They did do a good job on it though. How that happen anyway?"

I stared at him sideways, confused. His mom changed the subject.

"So, Shanell, have they given you any indication of how long you're gonna need to be here?"

I was still looking at Jay like he was crazy for asking that question. But then I turned my head in the direction of his mom and responded.

"None at all. I know I can't wait to get up out of this bed though. My body is all achy."

Jay looked me in the eyes as his arm was around me.

"Maybe they'll let me wheel you around in a wheelchair or something."

A grin appeared on his face as my eyes circled his. I smiled back, even though I couldn't pinpoint his behavior, whether he was mad at me still or if it was something more. He was certainly different.

"That would be nice, but I need a body massage." He gave me a devilish grin, first. "I'll gladly do the honors. Do I usually do stuff like that for you?"

"Oh, so now you don't remember that either?"

"I mean, it's a lot I don't remember, but I'm trying."

I moved my head back distancing ourselves, eyeing him again.

"Jay, don't gimme that. You remember everything."

"Yeah, that might've been true before."

"Shanell, did your mother get to talk to you about Jay's accident?"

My eyes darted at them both.

"What accident?"

"I'll tell her. You mind if we talk alone?"

"I'll be right outside."

"Jay, what accident?"

He changed his position now sitting opposite of me.

"I was performing at one of the shows, and I guess once I walked backstage and went down the stairs, I fell. Ended up hittin' my head."

My hand instantly cupped his thigh.

"Jay, that's not like you at all. Did you need stitches or anything or suffer a concussion?"

"Something like that. Stitches would've been better." His light eyes locked into mine with so much intensity. "I have something to tell you."

"Jay, you're scaring me."

"It seems since I've fallen, they're telling me I don't have all my memory back."

My mouth just hung open, speechless for a second. It just didn't seem real.

"... You... you don't have all your memory back? Is that what I just heard you say?"

"Look, Shanell, I hate to even say this to you, but I really don't even remember you right now. I'm only familiar with who you are because of what I've been told about you... well us."

In that moment, my breathing picked up rather fast. The man that I loved sat before me, not even knowing me. It broke my heart. I kept blinking, trying to prolong the tears that were soon to erupt.

"... You don't even know who I am?" My lips trembled. "You don't know me, Jay?" I cried. He looked at me like I was some pity case. It made me feel even worse.

"Please don't cry." He got up and grabbed some tissues then gave me one as he sat back down by me. "Look at it this way. Now that you're up, I can get to know you, and maybe that'll help with things. It's gonna be okay." He reassured me as he helped me to dry my eyes. I wished I didn't wake up. "Baby, I'm working really hard to try to remember things, but it's been hard." My intuition told me something was different with him, but this, I never expected. Even when Jay tried to comfort me, it felt forced, like he was comforting a stranger. It had no real feeling behind it.

"You... don't know... how much this hurts me right now," I stammered to get out.

"Unfortunately, you're right, and I'm sorry that I don't, but maybe you could look at it this way. We get to start all over."

"No, *you* get to start all over, Jay. I'm still stuck in the same place I was before, and that is loving you, and you don't even know me anymore."

"But I wanna get to know you. You my girl."

"I'm more than that!" I snapped.

"I'm not saying it like that to diminish who you are. I've been told who you are to me, but I needa feel that way again for myself."

That just got me more upset.

"And where does that leave me? Huh?"

His eyes drifted away from me before slowly returning the eye contact.

"I wish I could give you an answer right now, but I can't." I felt my lips quivering as I hurtfully gazed into his blank hazel eyes that peered back at me.

"You don't feel anything for me, Jay?"

His silence was deafening.

"Do you really want me to answer that right now?"

My tears soiled my face even more, leaving my skin saturated.

"You just did."

He stood up.

"Maybe I better go. I can't seem to do this right without making you cry."

I was at a loss for words, so I turned over on my side away from him. Ms. Murphy came back in the room after Jay came out. I was lying there in tears when she sat down beside me and tried to comfort me.

"It's gonna get better, okay, sweetie? We're all dealing with the same thing where Jay is concerned. He doesn't remember any of us."

I sat up to speak with her.

"He doesn't remember you either?"

She took my hand.

"Not at all. The doctor said his memory could come back right away, or it could take longer, so we're all waiting, sweetie."

A rush of relief came over me from knowing I wasn't alone.

"Oh, you don't know how good that makes me feel. Not that that's a good thing, but I thought it was just me that he didn't remember."

"No, it's not just you, if that helps you feel any better."

"Please know that I'm not happy that he doesn't remember you."

She covered my hand with both hers.

"Oh, I know that. I know what you meant by it... Look, you go 'head and get some rest, and I'm sure we'll be back up here soon."

"Okay."

After Jay and his mom left, Kelli came in the room to check on me. She walked in smiling and excited. I guess because Jay and I got to see each other, but she could tell I wasn't as happy about it like she was.

"Hey! I thought you would be all smiles seeing as though your man just left. Are you okay?"

"Not really. Kelli, does Jay know about the babies?"

"We were leaving that up to you or your mother to tell him, so if your mom hasn't said anything yet, then he doesn't know."

"Well I'd like for you to continue to keep that confidential. I'm not ready for anyone else to know."

"Of course."

"Thank you, Kelli."

"You don't have to thank me. How's your stomach feeling?"

"It's okay right now."

"Well, if you need anything let me know."

Just then, my mom walked in the room as Kelli was leaving.

"You just missed Jay's mom."

She gave me a kiss and then sat in the chair.

"How'd it go?"

"He doesn't even remember me."

"I know, sweetheart."

For some reason, I wasn't expecting her to say that.

"How come you didn't tell me he lost his memory?"

"I thought it might've been better if you heard it from his mom. I feel like that's all I've been giving you is news that you don't want to hear. I figured she could explain it better than me anyway, just in case you had questions."

"I'm not telling him about the babies."

That made my mom sit up even more in the seat.

"Shanell, why are you keeping this from him?"

"Mom, he doesn't even know who I am. How can I tell him he's gonna be a father?"

"Easy! You just tell him. It's not like he doesn't know you two have a past."

"He only knows what he's been told. He doesn't remember how deep that is. I would feel like I'm telling a person that I had a one-night stand with that I'm pregnant. I can't tell him until he remembers me and knows how much I meant to him."

"Shanell, I don't think you should wait to do that. What if he doesn't get his memory back or it's not until months from now? You'll be showing more than what you already are. You can't hide being pregnant, sweetheart. He's gonna know he's the father."

My hands clutched the blanket in anger.

"I'm not telling him right now. I'd also appreciate it if you didn't say anything either... to anyone!"

"Shanell—"

"I don't want anyone to know, Mom. It's my choice, and I don't want Jay or anyone else to know about it, okay?"

My mom's eyes bucked so wide, I'm sure from the way I spoke to her. I knew I was harsh, but she had to know how strongly I felt about this.

Chapter Three

FRICTION IN THE ROOM

*S*hanell

"I can't believe you're really keeping this from him." She folded her arms. "I don't like it." I leaned over in her direction and stared at her with a firm eye.

"Promise me, Mom, that you won't say anything."

"I think you're making a huge mistake."

"Mom, please promise me," I demanded.

"Fine, Shanell, but when this blows up in your face, I hope you're prepared to deal with it."

Jay

I told Nikki that I wanted to come to the doctor's appointment with her to see about the baby and talk to the doctor, so we were going today. Nikki's obstetrician was at the same hospital she worked at. Momma couldn't accompany me this time, because she had a speaking engagement of her own scheduled for the same timeframe.

I was okay with going alone anyway. Since we would be going to the same hospital that Shanell was in Sienna, Evan and Marcus wanted to go visit her while I was with Nikki. I met her at the hospital since she was already working. She told me to call her when I was in the lobby, and she'd meet me down there. The others went to go visit with Shanell except for Spence. He, of course, stayed with me. Nikki came down to the lobby dressed in her scrubs once I arrived.

"You ready?"

"Yeah."

"Hi, Spence."

Spence ain't like Nikki at all, but he decided to speak. He was seriously keeping his eyes on her.

"What's up."

Nikki led us to the elevators. Once our floor was reached, Nikki grabbed my hand with excitement, pulling me along. I could see Spence had a problem with her actions.

"Yo, Nikki! Won't you slow down wit' my man, alright. You got him here. He ain't going nowhere."

"Nah, she alright."

I saw a smirk appear on her face the moment I said that to Spence. We reached the OB/GYN wing and walked up to the desk for Nikki to check in. Then we all had a seat.

"So what's gonna happen when I go in here with you?"

"The doctor's gonna examine me and take a listen to the baby's heartbeat."

"Nikki Williams, you can come on back."

She grabbed my hand to get up with her. They told her to go use the bathroom and then she got her blood pressure and weight checked. Once that was done, we went in the room where she was told to undress from the waist down. While she was doing that, I was looking around the room at the pictures and diagrams of the babies in the womb. It was hard not to peek and admire her body as she changed, but I was tryna be a gentleman. I put my head down, but she raised my chin so I could look at her as she stood there in her panties and bra.

"It's okay. It's not like it's anything you haven't seen before."

"She said waist down. Why you take e'rything off?"

"Just easier." She smiled as she put on the gown. "Can you tie the strings?"

Her backside was putting on its own peep show, making me feel things I hadn't in a while. I tied her up quickly and went back to looking at the walls.

"Damn! That's what that looks like, huh."

"I know."

"Shit's incredible, man."

Nikki had just sat up on the table when her doctor walked in. She said hello to us and introduced herself to me.

"Oh! Would you happen to be the father?"

My eyes widened, caught off not really knowing what to

say, even though that likely was a possibility. Nikki spoke up for me.

"Yes, Dr. Gibson, he is. This is Jay Murphy."

"Are you that—" she waived her thought off "—no, never mind." Nikki and I knowingly stared at each other about who the doctor's first thoughts of me were. "Well, Mr. Murphy, I'm glad you could be here."

"Jay is fine."

"Well, Jay and Nikki, do you have any concerns?"

"Not that I can think of.

I looked at Nikki for a response since she would know more than me.

"Everything's been fine so far."

The doctor then went ahead and examined her in an area of my liking, but in this moment, it was less appealing. Then she put jelly on her belly and then this monitor that picked up a baby's heartbeat.

"That's it?" I asked.

"That's it," assured Dr. Gibson. "That's your little one's heartbeat."

"Oh my gosh! Jay, do you hear that? It sounds so strong. It's our little man."

"Somebody sounds confident. What if it's a girl?" asked the doctor.

"I know it's a boy. I can feel it," she exclaimed.

"Dr. Gibson, I have a question. How long does she have to wait before a DNA test can be performed?"

"Nikki is far enough now where one could be performed

on the fetus. Is that something that you guys want to set up?"
We both answered at the same time. Me saying yes and Nikki
saying no. The doctor stared at us, confused.

"Doctor, I just wanna know if I do this is it gonna harm
my baby? Wouldn't it be better to wait until after the baby is
born?"

"There are some risks involved when it's done during the
gestational stage. It is best to wait until the baby is born if
there's not a real urgency in my opinion. You both really just
want to consider the risks before you decide."

That made me contemplate the risks as I observed
Nikki.

"Well, if neither one of you have any more questions,
Nikki, I'll see you next month."

The doctor left out of the room, and Nikki started to get
dressed.

"Jay, I think we should wait to have the DNA test done."

"She didn't say we couldn't have it done. She just said we
needa weigh the risks. I think we needa see exactly what that
is first and then decide."

"I don't wanna risk losing our baby. Jay, we almost lost him
once."

"What you mean?"

She explained as she was getting her clothes back on.

"You don't remember this, but your best friend and I got
into a fight shortly after I found out I was pregnant. She
kicked me in the stomach, and we could've lost him. I was laid
up right here in this hospital."

"Hold up. Why you fightin' if you knew you was pregnant?"

"I wouldn't even say I was fighting. She came at me all of a sudden."

We were now standing in front of each other.

"I'm still gonna look into the risks."

"You do that, but I don't think I'm gonna have it done before this baby is born."

"Alright look, we'll finish this conversation later. You ready?"

"Yeah." Nikki got her appointment for the next month, and then we were rejoined by Spence.

"Jay, what are you about to do?"

"I'm actually about to go see Shanell. You mind showing me where to go?"

"I'd be happy to," she said with the biggest smile. "Follow me, gentlemen." She eagerly walked us to Shanell's floor. "You know where to go from here, right?"

"Yeah, I think we're good."

"Soo..." she sang as she happily twisted herself from side to side. "What are you doing later?"

"Not really sure."

"Well, if you wanna do something together, give me a call."

Spence nudged me.

"Come on, man. Let's go see Shanell."

Nikki bit the corner of her lip before smiling and turning to go on her way. I saw Spence shaking his head at her while she walked along. I went ahead in the room to see Shanell.

Spence ended up right behind me since he didn't watch her for any length of time. The moment Shanell saw us, she got happy for a moment, but then her expression changed.

Shanell

I was seeing Jay, but I knew he was not the same Jay. That tugged at my heart and diminished my happiness. There was an awkwardness now between us. Spence gave me a hug and a kiss on my forehead first. Then Jay followed and did the same, but he kissed my lips. That really surprised me.

"Come on, guys. Let's leave these two alone and give them some privacy. Shanell, we have a lot more catching up to do, girl."

"Aw, Sienna, I know. I really have missed you guys. Marcus, don't be mad at me okay?"

"Man, you starting to sound like a parrot to me... repeatin' the same ole shit."

He made me laugh.

"Marcus, you know I'm deeply sorry. Stop being like that."

They all hugged me and told me they'd be back to see me again before they dispersed. I gazed at Jay once the room was empty. We had this moment between us before Jay finally said something.

"So how you feeling today? You look like you're doing a lil' better... like you in better spirits."

My hands were crossed in front of my stomach on the covers.

"I feel okay. Where were you? The gang never said."

"Oh, I had to go with Nikki to her doctor's appointment."

My hands then fell to my sides as I was fueled with anger.

"You were with Nikki?"

"Yeah. You already know about the baby, right?"

That statement right there made me sit up and damn near come out of this bed and slap him shitless, because he was spewing a bunch of it as far as I was concerned.

"Are you serious?"

"Am I telling you something you didn't know already?"

"Of course, I knew! I just don't understand it. Why are you falling for her deception!"

"Look, I've already heard how I needa make sure this baby is mine and all that type of bullshit. I'm aware of that. But I'm not gonna turn my back on its mother just because I don't know that yet."

"I really don't believe I'm hearing this from you right now. Jay, this is Nikki! She has—you know what, do whatever you feel is best," I scolded, waving him off.

"How come I'm getting the feeling like every time I come see you it's gon' always be some bullshit?"

"Well maybe you shouldn't come and see me then if that's how you're feeling." Angrily, I folded my arms as my body jolted back against the pillow. He sighed heavily before taking a seat opposite of me again. I turned my head, not even able to look at him.

"This can't be how we used to be. I mean, when I look at us in pictures and shit, we looked like a happy couple. Why things feel so difficult?"

My eyes started to water and before long the tears were rolling down my face.

"They weren't always this difficult. What we have, I always thought no one and

nothing could touch it. You know why I felt that way, Jay?" I turned to finally face him. "It was because of you. You had this way of making me feel like out of all the women in the world, I was the only one that you had eyes for. Not only did you tell me that, but you would show me in so many ways. Now it's like we never meant anything to each other and can't even be in the same room without friction."

"I don't know how I can make you feel like that anymore. All I seem to do is make you cry."

"That's only because you don't remember what we had and how much I meant to you. That hurts so bad."

"Shanell, I'mma be straight up with you. I can't promise that I'm gonna get my memory back or even how much of it I'll get. Even if I do get it back, I can't promise you that what-ever I do get back that I'll be like I was before. I don't know who I was before. I'm just trying to be who I am right now, and who that is might not be who you want me to be. I really wish and hope that I can get back to being the man that made you feel like I was the one, but Shanell, what if I don't?"

I wiped my eyes.

"No, Jay, don't say that."

I found myself grabbing a hold of his shirt with both hands.

"Baby, I know that's not something you wanna face, and

honestly I hope we don't have to. I just don't want you tryna hold on to something and then become disappointed if you don't get what you hoped for."

"So are you giving up on us, Jay?"

His hands rested under my elbows.

"That's just it. I don't know anything about us. I just don't wanna keep hurting you until things come back."

"You won't." I whined as I held on tighter.

"I don't know, Shanell. I mean things are just too unpredictable right now."

I sniffled as I struggled to breathe and speak. My eyes were so heavy, just like my heart as I stared into the face of a stranger that didn't know me.

"So are you telling me we should call off the engagement?"

"That may not be a bad idea. I think maybe we should chill for a bit."

He shattered me.

"What!" I felt like my whole world just crumbled. I knew Jay didn't really know what he was feeling anymore because of the amnesia, but that didn't stop it from hurting. Out of nowhere, I gathered enough strength not to fall apart even more. I let him go, which in turn he released his hands from me. "I need to speak with Marcus. Can you ask him to come in here?" From the look on Jay's face, that request caught him off guard, but he did as I asked. He walked over to the door and asked Marcus to come in the room.

"Jay, can you leave us alone?"

Another unexpected request.

"Sure." Jay walked out. Now Marcus appeared baffled.

"What's goin on?"

"Everything! But that's not why I wanted you in here. Why wouldn't you guys tell me earlier why there's a cop outside of my door?"

Instantly, he got defensive. His eyes creased in the corners and his mouth was tight.

"Why you asking me?"

"Because I know you'll tell me. Marcus, really what's going on?"

He started rubbing a finger repeatedly up and down the back of his neck like he had a sudden itch.

"It's for security purposes."

"Because of my association with Jay?"

"Yeah."

"Well how come everyone else made it seem like it was this big secret and couldn't just say that?"

"We didn't know how you were gonna react to that, just coming out of a coma... shit could've frightened you or something."

I cracked up.

"Marcus, you're stupid."

"Nah, seriously though. We all just tryna look out for you. We didn't want you worrying."

"Worrying about what?"

"Okay, not worrying, but scared once you saw a cop at the door. You Jay's girl. Gotta have you secure."

"I don't know about that anymore."

"Aw, don't even gimme dat... You startin' already and just woke up." I laughed again. "So you cool now?"

"I'm trying to be."

"Tell them to slow down too on what they feeding you. Ya face getting chunky." That made me touch my cheeks.

"It is?" I panicked on the inside because of the pregnancy. "Oh, that's probably from the surgery I had on the scar. How does it look?"

"Gone." That made me grin. "How 'bout next time you let a nigga know?"

"I know, I know," I said, rolling my eyes away from him shamefully. "Marcus, how is Jay coping with all this?"

"He still tryna figure things out. We just gotta let him, you know?"

He sat opposite of me toward the end of bed.

"You knew he was with Nikki at that appointment, didn't you?"

"I did, but why would I tell you something like that?"

"Because I consider you to be more than my bodyguard, and I hope you feel the same."

"Most definitely. Look, don't even worry about Nikki. We got our eyes on her. Believe that shit."

"Well that's good to know. So what are you guys doing once you leave here?"

"I think we going to the house. Me and Evan just sticking close by Jay. Work's cut off for him until he can get back acclimated with a lot of things, so we just doing what he wants right now. Then we'll be back on Shanell patrol once you get out." He snickered as he patted my covered leg.

I smiled again.

"Okay. Well, I'm not going to keep you guys any longer. I see Jay keeps walking by the door. It was good seeing you though."

"You too, and awake finally. Now you gotta get outta here."

"I know. I'm working on it, believe me." Marcus gave me another hug. Suddenly, Jay came back in the room and saw our embrace.

"Y'all still talking?"

Marcus and I both looked at one another, taken by Jay's impatience.

"We're done, Jay. I didn't realize I was holding you up," I mentioned.

"Nah, I'm just surprised you two still talking, that's all. Everything alright?" he asked, eyeing us both. Marcus examined Jay and let out a chuckle.

"Man, why you bugging? What, you got a problem with us talking or something?"

"Nigga, go 'head with that."

"Jay, I said we're done," I stressed. "Marcus, thank you for answering my questions."

"Alright, Shanell."

"I'mma holler at her real quick, and then I'll be out there." Marcus nodded his head and then left out. Jay nervously rubbed his hands together as he stood over me.

"How come you couldn't ask ya questions in front of me?"

"Why does it matter? You wouldn't have known what they were about, not remembering anything anyway."

"I didn't ask you that. I just wanna know how come I had to leave the room?"

"What I had to say to Marcus had nothing to do with you, okay. And is that really why you interrupted us?"

Jay sat on the bed right beside me with a serious look on his face.

"I didn't like it."

"Me talking to Marcus?"

"It wasn't just you talking to him. You two just seem real friendly. I noticed it the first time I came in here with Spence and you were talking to him. What's up with that?"

"Okay, Jay, first of all, this is Marcus. You trust Marcus, but more importantly, you used to trust me. Now, I'm confused. One minute you're telling me let's chill, and now you're... doing this! Jay, what's going on?"

Jay leaned in and laid his head on my breast. I wasn't expecting that at all, but I just went with it and wrapped my arm around him and gently rubbed the top of his head.

"I don't know, Shanell. I just know something in me didn't like seeing you smile, and it wasn't because of me."

"Aw, babe, no one can put a smile on my face like you do. I know you don't know that for yourself right now, but I'm telling you. Jay, I love you so much. Baby, I know you're just trying to find your way, and I believe you will. I just hope and pray when you do, it will lead you back to me."

He looked up at me, and my heart just wanted to explode from being so full of love for him.

"I do too. I know I haven't said all the right things, and our situation isn't what neither one of us expected, but I hope the outcome works out for the best for both of us."

I heard Jay's words, and I knew even though he felt some type of way about my and Marcus's relationship, he still wasn't completely convinced about ours.

"I better get up outta here... got them waiting for me." He stood up. "I'll be back up here to see you though."

He kissed me so tenderly before he left out.

Chapter Four

BONNIE & CLYDE

*J*ay

Once I arrived home, I had a surprise there waiting for me. When I walked in, Momma and my aunt Pat and a beautiful young lady were all in the kitchen sitting at the table talking. I heard laughter, which was what made me walk in there.

"Aye! What's goin' on?"

I gave the family a hug and kiss and shook the young lady's hand as I said hello.

"Jay, you must don't recognize who this is then, do you?" Momma asked.

"Nah, but how you doing?"

"I'm doing fine." She got up on her feet. "Now I know you don't remember me, so I'mma tell you. I'm your best friend Lyric, and I'd like a hug more so than a handshake."

I glanced at her and smiled at the thought of her only being my best friend. She was too beautiful to be friend zoned. Had me curious about our relationship, but I did as she asked once I got out of my head.

"Oh, my bad."

I hugged her and then joined them at the table. Her tropical scent was still on me. She smelled good!

"I'm sorry to hear about what happened to you, Jay bear, but—"

"Jay bear?"

She had a dead ass straight face.

"Yeah! Jay bear. That's what I named you. Anyway, I think if I hang around you long enough, your memory will come back. We thick as thieves, so I'm sure once you can familiarize yourself with me, you'll remember," she said, confidently shaking her head.

"Word! That sounds like we used to get into some things."

"Used to? When we get together, we still do... good things of course," she clarified as her eyes roamed the table at everyone. They laughed.

"Can't nothing good come out of thieves being together." Lyric turned her attention to Momma.

"Mom, I think he's fooling us, 'cause he sure hasn't lost that sharp tongue of his." Momma just grinned at her.

"So how long we been best friends?"

"Since we were kids in grade school. Then my family moved away once we were in high school."

"Yes, Jay, you and Lyric seemed to get along with each

other as soon as you started playing together. Then after a while, her family had to move. You made me promise to let you keep in touch with her."

"That's interesting."

"No matter where we moved, our families made sure we stayed in touch. Then once we were old enough to travel, we saw each other on our own."

I nodded my head as I absorbed everything.

"Cool! So we got a lot of history together it seems."

"We became like Bonnie and Clyde, minus the lovers part."

"You two have been in each other's lives a long time," Momma concluded.

"Then once you started being all into girls, they'd see me and be jealous of our relationship. Some of them I had to put in their place."

"So you were the one that had the fight with Nikki?"

"Come on, Pat. Let's let them finish getting reacquainted."

"Honey, I was just sitting here watching the two of them, taking it all in," she said cheerfully. "Lyric, you know it's always a pleasure. It's some cobbler on the stove, Jay, if you want some."

"I knew I was smelling something good when I came in."

Momma grabbed my shoulders and kissed my cheek from behind before she and my aunt left the room.

"To finally answer your question, yeah, I beat her ass."

"But why would you fight somebody that's pregnant?"

"First of all, I didn't know she was pregnant. But she

needed her ass whipped for what she did to you. How do you remember that anyway, but nothing else?"

"Nikki mentioned it when I talked to her."

Lyric nearly popped a vein in her head the way her eyes tore into me. She leaned her body over the table, furious.

"When were you talking to her?"

"Today. I went with her to a doctor's appointment."

"Jay, don't tell me she still claiming she's pregnant and it's by you."

"She definitely pregnant. I heard the heartbeat today."

Hearing that made her fall back in the chair, leaving a draining expression on her face. This girl was dramatic.

"Are you for real?"

"Yeah."

"You say that like it's no big deal. Okay, let me keep in mind that you don't have all your memory right now, but Jay, Nikki is a liar."

"I already been schooled on her from Momma. I don't needa hear no more bullshit from you either about her. It's not about her. It's about the baby and the chance that it could be mine."

"Jay, that bitch... oops... where ya mom and 'em go?" She got up real quick to see if they were in hearing range then sat back down. "I'm cussing and what not... anyway, do you know that she drugged you to get you to sleep with her?"

"This girl don't look like she'd do some shit like that. No, she didn't."

"Yes, she did! You don't know everything that girl is

capable of. Yes, she drugged you." Then she whispered. "Fucked you, and purposely tried to get pregnant by *you*, which still remains to be seen."

"That ain't what she told me. It didn't happen that way."

"Negro!" she said, cuttin' her eyes at me. "How would you know what she told you was true anyway? Jay, don't listen to that girl. That bitch crazy! I'm sorry to be cursing so much, but I've never liked her. I always thought she was too obsessed with you."

"I don't know what to think, anymore... about any of this shit, really."

"Believe what we're telling you. She's been after you since you left her ass. Jay, you have Shanell now. She adores you. You asked her to marry you. That right there speaks for itself. You never thought you would be ready for marriage yet, but she changed all that for you."

"I told her I think we should chill on that for a bit."

Lyric's mouth dropped.

"You making me all kinds of irritated right now. Why, Jay?"

"I thought it was for the best. I mean, I can't marry some-body I don't even know anymore. I'm s'pose to have her waiting 'round until I find that out again?"

"You couldn't have at least waited until she got out of the hospital to say that to her?"

"I probably could've, but I honestly don't think it would've made a difference. It's like every time we talk, I always get her upset."

"Well what do you expect? She's just coming out of a

coma, trying to cope again. The love of her life doesn't know who she is, and then he tells her that he doesn't want to get married. That's a lot to deal with, Jay. I'm mad at you."

"Aye, it's a lot of that going around." I shrugged. "Get in line. Besides, I'm tired of people telling me how I needa feel about anybody. I'm tryna figure that out for myself."

"I'mma go and see Shanell tomorrow. You going?"

"She probably don't wanna see me. Nah, you go 'head," I encouraged.

"Why wouldn't she wanna see you? You betta go see her tomorrow. You don't have to come with me, but you need to go up there, Jay. I don't care if you keep getting her upset. You need to see her, and she needs to see you."

She had me thinking.

"I might go up there."

"Are you sure you got amnesia, 'cause you damn sure haven't forgotten how to be hardheaded... man! Alright, Jay bear, I'm about to head out."

I started laughing.

"I don't know how I feel about that Jay bear shit."

"That's what I've always called you, and you let me, and you *still will*."

"Yo' ass seem bossy."

"I'm not bossy. I just know what people need to do better than they do, especially when it comes to *you*." I laughed at her again. "Really, Jay, leave Nikki alone. You're gonna wish you had listened once you get your memory back. You watch. I'll catch up with you sometime tomorrow."

When she got up from the table, I did as well. I followed behind her as she walked to the door. Since I was told we didn't do handshakes, I gave her another hug, and then Lyric went on her way. Momma heard the door and came down the steps.

"Lyric left already?"

"Yeah."

"So did you two have a nice talk?"

"Yeah. She seem crazy."

Momma playfully tapped me on my chest.

"She ain't no crazier than you are."

"I like her though... She cool."

My eyes widened, and I shook my head as I thought about her.

"What?"

"I definitely didn't remember my best friend being a girl. Then again, having one never even crossed my mind."

"Well, does that surprise you?"

I looked over at Momma.

"No. Nah. I mean, I'm surprised we remained just friends as sexy as she is, honestly."

"Jaylen!" Momma yelled, eyeballing me.

"I'm not gon' try to talk to her or anything, but you can't help but notice how she looks."

"She is a beautiful girl, and to my knowledge you two have only been best friends to one another."

"Don't get me wrong, I'm not interested in changing that.

It just caught me off guard a little bit when I was told she was my best friend."

"Yeah, you guys are really close. Lyric's very protective of you, as you are with her. As you've grown into your career and having more and more women cross your path, she wouldn't hesitate to tell you about somebody she didn't like for you and why when you've talked."

"That's no surprise."

We both laughed.

"My point is, you always respected her opinion."

"I understand what you saying, Momma."

I followed her as she walked in the kitchen. I decided to eat some of the cobbler that was on the stove. She did too. We sat back down at the table and continued to talk. I had more I wanted to know about Lyric, my baby sis, and my career. Momma was very informative, and we ended up having a nice, long conversation. This was something we hadn't been able to do since my accident.

"Baby, I hope what we've discussed helps and gives you more clarity."

"It does help, Momma. Thank you!"

I got up from the table and took our dishes away. I left that table confused as shit, because everything seemed unreal, especially this Nikki shit.

Shanell

Kelli was just wheeling me back to my room after I had another ultrasound done. It left me very emotional. I had my first look at the babies, and to top it off I found out the due date was on Jay's birthday, August 28th. I was filled with so many mixed emotions. I didn't think I was ever going to stop crying.

Kelli was a life saver. I really enjoyed having her as my nurse. She was turning into a friend. We were around the same age, opposed to Mrs. Mable, so Kelli could relate to me, and I felt comfortable talking to her.

It wasn't a lot that I had to share, because Kelli was already privy to Nikki saying she was pregnant and the possibility of the baby being Jay's. She knew I was going through a lot and was always an ear for me whenever I wanted to talk. Once I got back in that bed, I felt drained. I had a little physical therapy also that morning, so it was catching up to me. Kelli gave me some tissues to dry my tears since seeing the ultrasound and a host of other things were bothering me, then she helped me get under the covers.

"Are you going to be okay?"

"Yeah, I'll be fine."

"Good. Just try to stay positive about everything, Shanell. God don't make no mistakes, so there's a reason why you guys are going through this. Girl, just ride it out. What don't kill you will make you strong. You both will be better for it."

"Kelli, me and Jay have been through so much already. I'm tired. It just has never been easy at all."

"Is anything worth having ever easy, Shanell?"

"No, but you just don't know all the constant shit that we have to battle."

"I don't need to know it all, but I know enough. I follow you guys. I've always been a fan of Jay's since day one. My point is, you're going to always have something being thrown at you. That's a part of relationships and life. But just like you got through those situations, you will get through this one. It may not seem like it right now, but this is a moment that's going to pass just like the others. Just hang in there, Shanell. He's worth having and so are you. He'll see that but you can't give up on him."

"He's given up on me."

"He don't know what he's saying right now." Suddenly, the police officer walked in the room and questioned me, making Kelli move out of the way. He showed me a photo ID.

"Do you know who this is?"

"Yes, I do. How'd you get that?"

"She's here to see you. How well do you know her?"

"Oh, very well. She's Jay's best friend. Is there a problem?"

"Not if she's someone you know. We can't be too careful. Do you want her in here?"

"Yes, of course."

"You sure you know her very well?"

"Yes, please... Let her in."

Lyric walked in the room, making Kelli's attention sway in her direction. She was a nice surprise.

"Ahh!" she screamed. "Oh my gosh! Hey, hun!"

She walked over and gave me the tightest hug.

THE COST OF LOVING YOU 3

"Mhm. It's so good to see you, Lyric."

Seeing her almost had me crying again.

"I also brought you some flowers too." She sighed. "But that cop still has them," she grumbled as she looked toward the door. Shortly after, they were brought in the room and sat on the table by the bed.

"These are beautiful! Thank you."

She plopped herself down in the chair.

"You're welcome. Okay, what was that all about? I mean, did they have to check the flowers though... damn!"

"That's Jay's doing. Making sure I'm safe."

"From who?" she asked, flaring her hands.

"Who knows... probably the paparazzi. You know how nosy they can be. Oh, Kelli, this is Lyric, Jay's best friend."

"Oh! Well, Lyric, it's nice to meet you."

"So how's she doing? When can she leave? It's like a damn prison in here."

"Well, she's getting better each day. Not sure when she'll be leaving though."

"'Cause ya boy 'bout to make me hurt him."

"Shanell, I'm going to step out for a bit so you two can talk. If you need anything, just use the call button."

"Okay! Thanks, Kelli."

"I see they did one thing right. Your face looks good."

"What'd you mean? What they do wrong?"

"Hello! The coma."

"Oh... right. Which you just reminded me... I still don't know how that happened."

"When you had your surgery done."

"I know that much, but why? What caused it?"

"Oh. I don't know. Good question."

"I've been so preoccupied. I haven't had a chance to really find out from anyone what caused it... hm... so anyway, what has Jay done for you to be ready to hurt him?"

"It's the way he's acting. I can understand it's because of his memory to a certain degree, but when you tryna tell the boy things we already know, you would think he would listen."

"You must be referring to Nikki."

"Girl, I feel like beating it in his head that he can't trust her."

"I know. So how did he react when he saw you?"

"He didn't know who I was either, but I'mma be here for a bit, and while I'm here I'm gonna make sure Nikki stays her ass away. She don't want no more."

"She's lucky I haven't seen her yet. I have some choice words for her myself."

"I would love to beat her ass again. She lucky she got that baby as an excuse right now."

"I know. Can you believe the nerve of her? She ain't really pregnant. I wish she'd stop with this charade."

"Jay said she was. He heard the baby's heartbeat at the appointment." That hurt like hell to hear.

"He did?"

My breathing began to pick up its pace.

"That's what he said."

"So... so... she's really carrying his baby?"

Lyric must've saw hurt all over my face, which made her rush to my side. The tears came rushing in as fast as she did.

"Shanell, I thought you knew the pregnancy was real, but we don't know if that baby is his though. You know how that girl lies."

"But she's really pregnant? He didn't even tell me."

"You didn't know he went to the doctor with her?"

"I did but... I guess it didn't cross my mind that he would be in the room with her and literally have proof. He heard a baby's heartbeat?"

"I'm so sorry, Shanell. I thought you knew all of this."

"He was supposed to experience that for the first time with me."

"Shanell, I'm really sorry. Hun, please keep in mind that this is Nikki we're talking about, and until you guys have proof, this child probably is not his."

"Jay seems to think it is, obviously," I muttered as I wiped my eyes. "He's actually getting into being a father, whether it's his or not."

"Okay, look, we're not going to do this. Stop crying! Nikki is not going to win here. Get yourself together so you can get out of this hospital and get back in ya man's heart. Crying and getting upset is not gonna fix things."

"I know. I just can't help it." I wiped my eyes again. "I feel like our life is falling apart, and the timing of it all couldn't be any worse."

"Well, we're not gonna let that happen. He belongs with you! I'm going to try my best to help make him see that."

Chapter Five

INTIMATE GATHERINGS

*J*ay

         I never did make it over to the hospital that day. Instead, I ended up being invited to a concert that K3 and Rich the rapper were having. I was down for some entertainment since I hadn't been out anywhere since the fall, so I got myself together and rolled out with Spence, E, and Marcus. They were performing at the *Apache Center*. K3 was in full effect.

Surprisingly, everyone was happy to see me. Even though I didn't remember who they were, I had no problem with chilling and getting reacquainted with folk while still keeping the amnesia low-key. There were swarms of women hanging 'round back in V.I.P., so I told the guys to relax and do their usual since everyone was just happy to see me. I was being stopped left and right by different ones showing me love that hadn't seen or spoke to me since the accident. Shit felt good!

I took a few photos with the ladies I conversed with. I kept things brief to not stir up any concerns. I was really enjoying this part of my life. I had a bottle in my hand, drinking as I talked to different people before I went to find a seat somewhere. It was nice chilling on the couch with ladies on each side of me. Some chick named Honey was sitting on one side but got up and left.

After Honey walked off, this other chick that was standing came over to me and sparked up a conversation. She told me her name was Val.

"How are you doing? Must be good since you're up and out."

"Yeah, I feel great!" I started asking her questions about herself, also talking about how pretty she was and how nice she looked.

"Will you stop," she babbled even though she enjoyed the compliments. She couldn't stop smiling at me. I got another bottle and shared it with her as we talked. She seemed to know a lot about me. Eventually, I got more comfortable with her and had my arm around her as we continued to talk, and I got acquainted with her.

"I have to be honest with you," she said while blushing. "You don't remember me, do you?" My eyes examined her face to see if anything would come to mind.

"Should I?"

"You've been interviewed at our company and have on occasion stopped at my job."

"Oh yeah?" I stated, minimizing my eyes, surprised. "Who you work for?"

"I currently work at *Lit Magazine*. I work the front desk."

"I can't say that I'm familiar."

"I understand. You had eyes for Shanell. It doesn't surprise me one bit that you've never noticed me before. Not that you've seen me as often as I've seen you."

That made me unwrap my arm from around her and put the bottle I had in my hand down.

"I actually was talkin' 'bout not being familiar with the magazine, but you know about Shanell, and you let a nigga have his arms all around you and flirting and shit with you?" I questioned, looking at her curiously.

She laughed it off like it was nothing.

"I was going to call you on it eventually. I wanted to see how far you'd go, but we'll keep this our little secret. It surprises me though that you're not familiar with the name of the company she works at or even where you've been interviewed. You might want to lay off the drinks."

"Oh, so you blaming it on the alcohol?" I looked at her sincerely. She thought that was funny for some reason. "Recently, when I had my accident, it fucked my head up a bit. I'm struggling to remember a lotta shit. Things get mixed up sometimes, so excuse me if I'm not familiar."

She put her manicured hand on my knee and stared at me, concerned.

THE COST OF LOVING YOU 3

"Jay, I'm sorry. I had no idea it was that severe. How is Shanell by the way? I feel so horrible about what happened to her as well. They were only letting family see her the last time I checked."

"She's out of her coma now. If you work with her, you should go see her."

She gave me a partial smile.

"I may just have to do that. She's been missed at work." She patted my leg. "Well, I have to go. A friend of mine has arrived. Would you excuse me?"

"Not at all."

"Good seeing you, Jay. Take care of yourself."

When Val left, another female that recognized me came over and sat beside me and hugged me before she started talking like I knew who she was.

"I'm so glad to finally see you. I've missed you so much!" She let me go and smiled. "It's good to see you. You don't know how happy I am that you're okay."

"You are?"

She placed her hand on her hip and leaned back.

"Jay, it's me, Autumn."

"Autumn, just do me a favor and refresh my memory on how we know each other."

I sat back and relaxed as she spoke.

"Are you serious?"

I smiled at her and gave her a head nod.

"Humor me."

"Jay, I'm always at your shows. I was just with you when

you opened for Acqwon... the night of your accident."

"You were with me?" I said pointing inward.

"Well, I wasn't with you, so to speak, but I was there. I've actually been to all the shows that you were on with Acqwon during that tour."

"So besides ya beautiful face, what other reason should I have for remembering
you?"

"Well, for starters, we would talk from time to time like we are now because I would always have access backstage and in the intimate gatherings that you guys would have."

"Nah... I can't say I remember any of that."

"Really? Is that a result from your fall?"

"Yeah... you could say that. It's some things I don't quite remember yet."

"I guess you don't remember me kissing you either then."

"Nah, baby. Not that a kiss from you may not be memorable, but I can't say that I do."

"I could tell because you didn't even say hi to me or give me a hug like you usually do. I thought you were mad at me at first."

"What would I be mad at you for?"

"For the kiss."

"Why would a kiss from a pretty girl as yaself make me mad?"

"Did you forget about Shanell?"

"No! Never! When did we kiss?"

"I kinda took advantage of a situation when you were in

Breah doing a show. That night when you performed, there was a group of us waiting backstage to see you. You were nice enough to talk to us for a minute. One of the girls asked you how was Shanell. You said there had been no change in her condition. You looked so lost when that question was asked. I just wanted to comfort you, so I kissed you, just letting you know things would be alright."

"If you got the impression that it meant anything, I can't real—"

"No, no... I got the picture after you pushed me away and left so abruptly. I really felt bad about kissing you, after the fact of course. I knew the pain you were feeling for not being able to be there for Shanell. I... I just wanted to make you feel better."

By now, Autumn had her legs across my lap as she filled me in on those past events. Not once did I give thought to the fact that I was ever unfaithful to Shanell. It made me wonder if I had done something more with anybody else.

"It's all good, baby. I just have to be more careful with the situations I'm in."

Marcus

"Yo, Spence, E, check that out over there."

They both looked over and saw what I did.

"He's too damn cozy with her," Spence observed.

"I say we put an end to this right now. He looks like he's had way too much to drink," said E. We weren't too far away from Jay, so we stepped over to 'em.

"Yo, man, you 'bout ready to roll?"

He looked at me, laughing. He was feeling it by now.

"Nah, I'm good. What y'all niggas doing?" Jay asked as we all stood surrounding him. "'Cause I'm in the middle of something."

Spence got stern.

"I can see dat, but I think it's time to go. Got things to do in the morning," he cautioned.

"Nigga, we don't got nothing planned." Jay stood up. "I make the plans, remember. Besides, I'm tryna chill with this beautiful young lady." I turned my head in her direction. "Baby, what's ya name?"

"Autumn." She smiled graciously at the three of us. E intervened.

"Autumn, you mind if we speak to him alone?"

"Sure!"

She started to get up.

"No!" Jay put his arm in front of her, stopping her from walking away. "She don't hafta go nowhere. What da fuck is wrong wit' y'all?"

Spence got angrier.

"Nigga, she don't, but you do. You don't need no extra shit poppin' off for the paparazzi to chew on."

I agreed.

"He's right, man. I think it's time for you to go too."

"Y'all niggas crazy. I'm just tryna have a good time tonight."

"Aye, Autumn, Jay gon' get up with you another time," Spence asserted. "Let's go!"

Jay

He led the way for me to follow him out. I knew I was a little buzzed; that was why I didn't put up too much of a fuss. We made a stop at the gas station on our way home. Spence went inside the store to buy something to munch on. I had my head resting back chilling, as I enjoyed the night air until I heard females laughing. That made me pop my head up, and I noticed Nikki was one of them.

She was standing on the passenger side of a car talking to the girl she was with while her friend went to pump the gas. Then Nikki got back in the car. She didn't even notice the car since we were in a different ride, nor did she see Spence. I made it my business to get out the car and walk over there. I noticed Marcus was watching me.

"Jay, man, where you going?"

"I'll be back. I'm just walking right there," I explained, pointing in that direction. Her friend spotted me and spoke.

"Hey, Jay."

"Aye! Baby, lemme get dat for you."

I finished pumping the gas for her. She went and got back in the car since she saw Nikki getting out to talk to me.

"Tonight's turning out to be a great night. That's nice of you to do."

She was all smiles standing there.

"What you doing out here this late?"

"I was at the show, then we stopped to get something to eat and now gas."

"Don't you think you needa hold off on shows and that type of shit for a while?"

Nikki moved in close, bringing her face up to mine.

"Are you saying that as the concerned daddy?" I put the gas pump back on the holder and didn't even respond to that question.

"She 'bout to take you home now, right?"

"Probably. I don't know what we're about to do. Why?"

"'Cause you needa have yo' ass in the house."

"Why? Because I'm pregnant?"

"Yeah! What's out here this time a night?"

"Well, I bumped into you," she said playfully.

"I ain't carrying no baby either." She was starting to get under my skin. "Look man, won't you go home."

She linked her arm in mine.

"I'll go home if you come with me?"

Spence came over to us since he saw me.

"Come on man. Let's go.'

"I think I'mma get dropped off at her place."

Spence shook his head and sighed.

"Jay, man, I think you should go home." Nikki annoyingly fixed her eyes on Spence since she had a problem with him telling me that.

"I'm just gon' chill at her house for tonight. Plus, I needa talk to her."

Spence just shook his head disapprovingly again. I got back in the car. Once everyone was in, the driver followed behind her friend as she dropped Nikki off. We pulled up to her house. Spence sighed then looked at me firm.

"Jay, we'll be back here first thing in the morning."

"I'll be ready, man. Chill."

Nikki was impatiently waiting for me to get out of the car until she saw the door finally open. I followed her into her house and plopped down on the couch with my whole body stretched out on it. Suddenly, one of my phones started to go off. When I answered it, it was Autumn. I sat there and talked to her for a minute. Nikki was staring at me the whole time with her arms folded and an attitude, even though the conversation wasn't long.

"I just wanted to make sure you all made it home and you were okay. The fellas were really upset with you."

"E'rything cool. I'm good."

"So are you busy?"

I looked over and saw how Nikki was staring me down like it was a contest.

"I am, actually, but how'd you get my number?"

"Jay, you must be wasted. You gave it to me tonight, finally."

"Well, I'mma hit you back then, alright?"

"I'd like that."

"Later."

"Yo' ass ain't calling her back while you're with me, so don't tell that bitch that." I looked at Nikki, displeased with her sudden outburst and uncalled for foul language.

"Fuck's ya problem?"

"Who was that?"

"Why? I was hanging up. You ain't have to holla and say all that bullshit."

"You ain't have to answer that *either*!"

"I'm sorry, alright?"

"You better be."

"Damn, baby, why so hostile... nigga apologized."

"Because you're with me right now." She walked to the couch I was on and scooted my legs over so she could have some room to sit beside me. "I'm sorry, but you need to turn those phones off."

"Nah, I can't do that."

She tried to take the one I was just on out my hand but couldn't. Nikki was really tripping tonight, which made me remember that I had some more questions about us sleeping together.

"Yo! Chill wit' dat shit!"

"Well, can you not take any more calls please?"

"Lemme ask you something. I keep hearing you drugged me to have sex with you. Is that true?"

"What? Who told you some mess like that?"

"Is it true?"

She stood up like she was offended.

"Do I look like I would need to do something like that to you?"

"That's not an answer."

"No, Jay. I would never harm you in any way. I love you."

"I just find it strange to be hearing stuff like that about you."

"I don't." She sat back down. "It's a lot of people that don't like me because I used to be with you. People are jealous. They'll say anything to turn you against me. Oh, and if you heard this from your best friend, she hates me anyway."

"Why would you assume I heard it from her?"

"I know she's here in town, and one thing for certain, she better stay away from me."

"Look, she ain't here to cause no problems. I wouldn't let that happen anyway." I squirmed around to get a little cozier on the couch. "Where I'm sleeping?" I asked as I stretched closing my eyes. "Nigga tired."

"Upstairs with me."

"I think I'mma just chill right here... shit... I can't even move."

"No, Jay, come upstairs with me."

I didn't hear nothing after that. I was out.

"Jay!"

She startled me, making me pop my head up.

"What? What's wrong?" Nikki started pulling my arm and shit.

"No. I can't let you sleep down here on this couch. You need to be comfortable."

"Nah, baby, I'm good," I urged, shrugging her off. "Go on to bed."

She didn't like that shit. She wanted me in her bed, but I was good where I was and dozed off again.

. . .

Nikki

There was no way I was letting him leave my house without getting something out of it. While Jay was sleeping, I quickly went upstairs, freshened up and got comfortable. I came back down the stairs in my panties and bra. I watched him for a minute as he lay there asleep. It didn't seem real that he was here, in my presence, right in my living room. Carefully, I kneeled beside him on the couch and unfastened his pants.

Jay

I was still sleeping until I felt this wetness on me, pleasuring my shit. I looked down, and Nikki's mouth was going to work, giving me some serious head. My body was stuck at a halt to the feeling from the initial shock. Then, as I watched her take me in deeper and deeper, that shit got me more aroused. I grabbed the top of her head, guiding it as I helped her to take me in.

The warmth of her hand wrapped around my dick while it was submerged in her wet mouth had my shit like a brick. My body gyrated as the pleasure became more intense. My mind was fucked while she was doing this, and I was enjoying it too much to stop her. I continued to groan, and as she handled my dick, I forced it more on her, letting her know this shit felt amazing.

Nikki

I did as I was commanded. All I ever wanted to do was

please this man and love him, and by the sounds he was making and the looks he was giving, I damn sure was doing my job. Looking at Jay's face as he attacked my throat, punishing it, I loved it. I made me want to suck his bottom lip too as it protruded out as he moaned, but first thing first.

Jay was finally ready to bust. I held his pole close, smearing his eruption on my lips, coating them before I swallowed his seeds into my mouth. He was trying to pull away, but my jaw game was too good and wouldn't let him. I blocked his hand and drank all his warm sweetness as he saw me savor him. He was still trying to calm himself.

"Mm. I love how you taste. I missed that."

His breaths were hard.

"Da fuck I do to deserve dat shit! Damn!"

"That's how naughty Nikki gets down, but I'm sure you wouldn't know nothing 'bout that waking up to Shanell."

Jay

I wasn't even thinking about Shanell, until now.

"Why you gotta bring her up?"

"Because I don't know why you're even with her when deep down inside, you know I'm the love of your life, and can't no one love or fuck you better than me. I will always love you, Jay."

I fixed my pants then made her move out the way as I got up off the couch.

"Where ya bathroom?"

"It's the door right there."

I walked in there. She had me annoyed now for some

reason. Once I came out, Nikki wasn't around, so I figured she must've gone upstairs. I laid back down on the couch in thought. Then here came Nikki shortly after.

"You don't wanna come upstairs with me?"

"Nah, I'm good."

"Then I'll just sleep down here with you."

Nikki laid on top of me and snuggled her head under my neck.

"Won't you go on and get in the bed? You can't be comfortable laying like this."

"The only way I'm going to bed will be if you come with me." I sighed first, tired. She wouldn't leave it alone about me going upstairs. I finally went up there and laid down with her. She wanted to fuck and started kissing on my neck. At first, I laid there quietly and just let her. She crawled on top of me and started pulling up my shirt so she could kiss on my chest. I was with it at first, but then I stopped her.

"Nah. I can't do this." I pulled my shirt back down on me.

"Why?"

"What about the baby?"

"Jay, we can still have sex. It's not gonna hurt anything... Please, baby, make love to me. I wanna feel you inside of me again." Nikki started pulling up my shirt again, desperately trying to get it off. I didn't like all her aggression and grabbed her hands.

"Yo! Chill for a minute."

"But I want you."

"I get that. I need a minute. Relax!"

Nikki laid back beside me, wanting me to hold her then. Truthfully, I didn't feel like it, but I did it anyway. My mood had suddenly changed. Nikki ended up waiting so long she fell asleep. I couldn't sleep. As I laid there, I was suddenly filled with thoughts of Shanell.

I knew it had to be something special about her that captured my heart since I asked her to marry me, but I still was confused about where Nikki fit into all of this. Why was I still fooling around with her?

The next morning, Spence came early and picked me up. Nikki never even knew I left because she was still sleep. Once I got home, I ended up going back to sleep. I slept for another four hours and then he woke back up, took a shower, and got dressed. Momma was the only one still staying at my place since my aunt and Janae left. Janae had to go back to school, so my aunt was going to be with her while momma stayed with me.

She had made some breakfast for me before she was on her way out. I came down the stairs and got to spend a few quick minutes with her before it was time for her to go.

"And where were you last night?"

"K3 had a show, so we went there."

"Did you stay at a hotel?"

"No."

"When are you going to go visit Shanell again, Jay?"

"I was actually thinking about going to see her today."

"Baby, I know this has been hard on you having to adjust to things and get to know people all over again, but please keep in mind that you and Shanell were building a life together. You may not have your memory right now, but she still has hers, and a lot of that consists of you. Don't forget about her, okay?"

"Nah, I wouldn't do that. Obviously, not intentionally. I'm just taking my time with things."

"Well, I gotta go. I'll see you later."

Momma gave me a kiss and then left out of the house. Right when she left, my phone rang.

"Hello."

"I missed you this morning. How come you didn't tell me you were leaving?"

"I didn't wanna disturb you."

"Well I had a nice time last night."

"Oh yeah?"

"Mhm, so when can we do it again? I believe it's something else you still owe me."

"You tell me."

"If you were still here you could've had more, and so could I."

"Yeah, well hold that thought." I caught a glimpse of a picture of Shanell and me sitting on top of the bar in the sunroom I was eating my breakfast in. This was one that I hadn't seen already. "Lemme call you back."

"When, Jay?"

"Look, I gotta go. I'mma call you back."

I hung up from Nikki and walked over and picked up the photo. It had me wondering if maybe Momma had it. It was a picture of me sitting at a dinner table somewhere, and Shanell was standing behind me with her arms around my neck as we laughed. I just couldn't understand why I still couldn't remember anything about her.

The man in the picture had the biggest smile on his face, and Shanell was cracking up. I didn't know what about, but they looked like they were having fun, happy, and very much in love. I decided to go over to the hospital and spend the day with her. Like Lyric said, if I made her upset, then I would have to deal with it. Maybe I did need to see her more to remember again.

Chapter Six

CIRCUMSTANCES

*J*ay

Spence and I went over to the hospital. We stopped to talk to the cop first.

"Just curious, but has there been any new developments in Shanell's case?"

"Not as of yet. We're still going through all the people that worked there that day and had appointments scheduled. We've also noticed that the threat letters haven't showed up lately. We're wondering if it's because the culprit knows that Shanell is in the hospital, so we're watching to see if a pattern develops, but if anything, new turns up, I would be sure to let you know, Jay."

I'd been thinking about so much other shit lately, I hadn't thought about the fact that someone was tryna kill Shanell.

"Spence, does she know what's going on?"

"Nah, man. She has no idea."

"Let's keep it that way then. One less thing she has to worry about while she's in here recovering. So, tell me this then. What's the reason she thinks the cop is outside her room?"

"She thinks it's because of her association with you and to also keep the paparazzi out."

"Cool. That's decent enough then."

"You good, man?" asked Spence.

"Yeah. Let's go in."

I had my mind made up that I was going in this room and make this a good visit between us, no matter what. When we walked in, Shanell was on the phone talking to someone. I could tell she was surprised to see me. Spence went ahead and sat down while I just stood beside her with my hands in my pockets. As Shanell brought the call to an end, she told whoever it was that she loved them and then she got off the phone.

"I hope we didn't interrupt anything."

"No, it was my dad on the phone."

I felt kind of awkward, but I went ahead and put my arms around her to hug her. She reciprocated.

"How you doing, Shanell?" asked Spence.

"I'm actually not feeling very well today. Having a hard time keeping anything down."

"May I?"

I wanted to take a seat beside her.

"Sure!"

I could see it in her face that she wasn't feeling well. It had me concerned.

"You still having that nauseous feeling?"

She pursed her lips together and breathed out heavily before responding.

"Yeah."

"Do they know what's causing it yet?"

"I know what's causing it... It's this food."

I laughed, but she didn't.

"Maybe I should've called you first... checked to see if you needed anything."

"I want some surf and turf, like steak, steamed shrimp, lobster tail, mashed potatoes on the side with broccoli."

"You might wanna hold off on eating that if ya stomach bothering you. You probably need some soup and crackers... something light like that."

She bent her head down and rolled her eyes up and held that position for a few seconds.

"I don't wanna see no more soup. I get enough of that with this menu."

"Maybe I'll surprise you with something later." Now she was looking at me with her eyebrows raised and her eyes all bugged up. "Why you fixin' ya eyes at me like that?"

"It's nothing. So how have you been?"

"I'm doing alright, considering things."

"Have you had any signs of remembering anything?"

"Nothing yet."

"Oh... Lyric came to see me."

"Let me take this," said Spence. "I'll be back."

He had a call and got up to leave out of the room.

"Yeah, she told me she was coming up here. That's good. I'm glad you got to see her. She's been helping Sienna with a few personal things."

"I heard you got to listen to the baby's heartbeat."

My eyes instantly focused on the floor. I couldn't bear to see her face when she made it very clear the last time how she felt about my seeing Nikki. I really didn't want to talk about her with Shanell, but I answered her.

"Yeah. I got to hear it."

"So how did you feel when you heard it?"

Another question I didn't wanna answer, but I looked at her and told her the truth.

"I mean, it was incredible... to know that's a brand-new life about to begin..." I pondered on that for a second. "Yeah..." I shook that thought off. "But I didn't come up here to see you and talk about that. I wanna concentrate on us," I stressed as I took her hand in mine.

"Us, Jay? Is there an us?"

"I'm talking about me and you, in this moment, right now."

Shanell abruptly moved her hand away and grabbed the basin that was on the tray by her and threw up in it. I took it out her hand and held it for her. She laid her head back on the pillow once she was done. I went to go empty it in the bathroom.

"Jay, could you get something to drink for me please? Mrs.

Mable should be out at the desk." She was, and she gave me a small can of ginger ale soda to give to her. I opened it and handed it to Shanell. She took a sip and set it back on the tray and relaxed again.

"Ugh! I can't take this feeling."

"What you have to eat today?"

"Just what they gave me for breakfast, but even liquids barely wanna stay down."

"I'll be back."

"Jay, where are you going?"

"To talk to the nurse."

She suddenly leaned forward.

"About what?"

"About you! See if they can give you something."

"No! It's fine. It's just my body adjusting to the changes... with the coma and everything."

"How you know that?"

"It is, Jay... look! I'll be fine."

"I'm just tryna make sure."

A few minutes later, the doctor comes in the room.

"Hello. Jay, right?"

"Yes, sir."

"I just recently found out that my wife is a fan of your music. I had no idea who you were when we first met."

"It's all good. Maybe I could give her an autographed CD, or is she one that downloads music instead?"

"An autographed CD would be perfect. Thank you!"

"No problem. I'll leave it with Shanell the next time I come back."

He walked over to her.

"Well, that's why I'm here. Shanell I have some good news for you today."

"Okay."

"You'll be released... oh, excuse me. It seems I'm being paged. I'll be right back." He left out. Shanell had a downward gaze, holding her hands in her lap.

"You hear that? You finally get to come home."

"Jay, before you had your accident, I was going to be moving in with you, but now when I get out of here," she held her head up, "I'm going to stay at my condo. I think that would be best."

Little did she know, I was not having that. Even though I knew things weren't the same with the two of us, I wasn't going to let her be alone, knowing someone was after her.

"No. I think you needa come back to the house. You're just getting out of the hospital, Shanell. You don't needa be by yourself. Lemme take care of you."

"I don't need you to take care of me because of that. I need you to want to take care of me because you remember that's what you used to do. What *we* used to do for each other."

"There you go being difficult. It's not about what *I* or *we* used to do for each other. It's about now, and right now, I think we should stick with you coming to the house."

She folded her arms as she took a stand.

"I'm not staying there, Jay. I just can't!"

Then Dr. Mitchell returned to the room.

"Sorry about that. Okay, as I was saying, Shanell you're going to be able to go home real soon. We need to have a few things in place first. Because of your condition, it hindered you from doing your physical therapy as intense as we would've done normally. You need to continue with that. We can have a physical therapist come and work with you or you can go to a facility. Under the circumstances, we thought you'd prefer being home."

"Doctor, is there any particular equipment she needs to have if she did it at home?"

"No, they're going to basically work on her leg. My concern is it could take a lot out of her energy wise, so she'll probably be real tired. We just want her to be as comfortable as possible. Another thing is we're going to have a visiting nurse come for the first few weeks to check on her vitals. Shanell is still considered high risk, so we want to keep a close monitoring on her."

"Well, since she's considered high risk, is it best for her to leave right now?"

"Yes, we can keep an eye on her condition this way, without her having to spend the next several months in the hospital. It's more comfortable for the patient that way too. If anything arises, we'd be aware of it and if necessary, bring her back, but right now, there's no real concern to keep her here."

"Okay, Doc."

"Now the address that was provided when you were

admitted, Shanell," he said as he looked in her file. "Is this where we should have the nurse and therapist come?" He showed Shanell the file with the address on it.

"No."

"Lemme see that." I wanted to see what the address was she used initially. After I saw it, I gave Dr. Mitchel a different answer. "Yes, that address is correct. That's where they can come." The doctor looked at Shanell, but I got his attention back. "That's my home address. That's where she'll be at."

"Okay. Well I'll get all this set up, and Shanell, I'll be signing off on your release papers once that's done, and you guys will be good to go within the next day or so."

"Thanks, Doc... Oh, and I'll have that autographed CD for your wife before she gets up outta here, too."

Dr. Mitchell shook his head okay.

"Thank you, Dr. Mitchell." He waved to Shanell as he left out. She was staring at me mad afterwards.

"Don't look at me like that. Yeah, I said it! You coming back to the house with me. I'm not letting you go back to the condo by yaself... You can be mad with me all you want."

"I won't be by myself. My mother and Nevaeh are there."

"Yeah, for how much longer though?"

"I don't have the energy to argue with you, Jay, so for now I will go. But I'm not staying there long."

I sat back beside her on the bed and got close to her face and smiled.

"You were going anyway."

She was trying so hard not to laugh because she wanted to

be mad with me, but she couldn't hold it in any longer and smiled too.

"You get on my nerves! You can be so silly at times, you know that?"

"At least I finally got you to smile."

She didn't say anything for minute, but the love that emitted from her eyes spoke volumes.

"You've always had the ability to make me smile, Jay, even when I'm laid up in the hospital. It always amazes me how you bring so much light to dark situations."

"You been in here a lot?"

"It feels like it. You asked me how I got that scar on my face. An ex-boyfriend of mine did it several months ago."

"So that happened while we were together?"

"Yeah. It actually happened while we were at my house. I have one that I rent out. My ex never got over the fact that we were together, and I didn't want him anymore. He came there looking for me... Basically, he got upset when he realized you were there. He had me tie you up—"

"Hold up! How were you able to tie me up without me getting in his ass?"

"He had a gun to my head, Jay. You didn't want to risk my life." That shit through me for a loop. "So when I tied you up, he of course went behind me to make sure I tied it was tight enough and I wasn't trying anything sneaky. Then... I don't know... he got real agitated with me and grabbed a knife and cut me."

"Damn, baby... I'm sorry that nigga did that to you. I couldn't do anything to help you?"

"No, but you tried to so bad. It just was a bad situation. Thank God my girlfriend Val was on her way over to bring me some paperwork that I'd forgotten at work. She got suspicious when I didn't come to the door and called the cops. Plus, she saw you were tied up." That made me think about our encounter the other night. She got real cozy with me. Even though she said she wasn't the best of friends with Shanell, but the fact that she came by to bring her work and called the police made me think she was closer to her than what she let on. I wondered if she would tell Shanell how I was flirting with her.

"Jay?"

"I'm sorry. I just was tryna digest everything. Did he just leave us there...? Like, what happened?"

"No, the cops caught him still in the house. I was knocked out because he had pistol whipped me, since I was screaming, and it was making him crazy from what you told me. He was just holding me on the floor stroking my hair when the cops busted in."

"I would end up going to jail for killing his ass if I ever saw him again."

"Yeah, well you came pretty close to it, but he's in jail as of now anyway."

"Nigga needa be under the jail."

"El has caused a lot of drama for me and you. He came

after me again when I was back home in *Kilborough* visiting my parents."

"This bitch nigga needa be handled."

"I got into a car accident trying to get away from him then. Ended up breaking my leg, which is why I have to do physical therapy now." I had so much going through my mind from everything that she was telling me. "Jay, are you remembering anything?" My mind was racing from her speaking of Val, to this shit with Nikki, and the sucka ass that El was. It made me remember something. "Jay, are you okay?"

"Yeah. I just had this picture in my mind, of a cast on ya leg, and I'm helping you get dressed in the bathroom somewhere."

"Yes!" she said, excited. "That was in the hospital. You did! You helped me get dressed in the bathroom since I couldn't do it myself, because I was still in a lot of pain."

"Yeah that shit just came to me outta nowhere."

"Oh my gosh! Jay, you're starting to remember things."

"That was the first time that's happened, but I'm not gon' get my hopes up yet over one thing, you know. That was a nice little memory though. I just hope more and more keep coming to me."

"Well, that's a start, right? It's just gonna take some more time."

It seemed I really did need to be around her, for more reasons than one.

Chapter Seven

DISRESPECTFUL

*S**hanell***

The day came for me to finally get out of the hospital. My mom and Nevaeh were over Jay's house, waiting for our arrival. I was so happy to be leaving and up out of that hospital bed. I got hugs from everyone once I walked through the doors. I really didn't know what to do with myself. I wasn't too pleased to be staying here right now, but I told Jay I would, but in my mind, it would only be for a short period of time.

"Shanell, can I offer you something to eat? I know you 'bout tired of that hospital food," his mom asked.

I was hungry since my hospital diet had me eating very clean. I truly was ready for something new. They had food prepared for me. It was a brunch. My mom pulled me to the side.

"Are you sure you're going to be able to eat without getting sick?"

"At this point, I don't even care."

Everything looked good, and I was so hungry for something substantial. I quickly went to take a seat. As we sat in the kitchen and ate, I noticed my mother was closely watching me as I consumed my meal. After a while of talking and trying to find a bit of normalcy in an extraordinary situation, I had to go to the bathroom.

As I got up, I noticed Jay was on his cell phone standing in the foyer. He didn't see me at first because his back was turned. I heard him say Autumn, which was unusual. Honestly, I didn't know what to make of it, but I most certainly was curious. Jay heard me and turned around. I just proceeded to go to the bathroom. Once I came out, Jay was no longer on the phone. He noticed my unfriendly facial expression and knew something was up.

"What's wrong with you?"

I decided to ask him who it was instead of letting him know I heard the name, just to see if he'd tell me.

"Was that a female you were just on your phone with?"

"Shanell, she was only inviting me to this club, and I told her I didn't know if I was gonna go. That's all it was."

"Oh, so we're giving females the number now?"

"Look, can we talk about this later? I don't wanna do this why we got people here."

"You didn't mind talking on the phone while they were here, but I have to wait?"

He clinched his jaws together as if my questioning was bothering him.

"Okay, can we at least go talk in private?"

Shortly after, Nevaeh walked out there with us.

"Hey. Your mom wanted me to check on you." She suspiciously stared at the both of us before looking back at me. "You guys okay?"

"I'll be downstairs if you need me." Jay walked away. That did it for me and pissed me off!

"Nevaeh, I can't do this. I can't stay here with him."

"Why... what happened? Wait! First, just go upstairs. I need to tell Auntie something so she's not worrying about you, and then I'll be up there."

"Yes, let her know the food is staying down just fine."

Nevaeh went in the kitchen to give my mom some excuse as to why I wasn't back yet, but she told her I was okay. Then she ran upstairs to talk to me. She found me in the master suite sitting on the bed.

"Cousin, what happened?"

She sat down beside me.

"He's talking to other people already."

Her eyes searched my face with wonder.

"Who?"

"I don't know. Some girl named Autumn. I heard him on the phone with her."

"What did he say?"

I looked at her from the corners of my eyes.

"Does it really matter? He shouldn't be talking to her in

the first place."

"Maybe it was business."

She knew by the way I eyed her that answer wasn't fore-seeable.

"No, Nevaeh. She was inviting him to a party."

"I see me and Jay are about to fight now."

Hearing him speak to another woman on the phone made me feel so disrespected.

Grant it, he didn't have his memory, and we hadn't had the best communication since, but seeing him not give a damn about me was breaking my heart.

"Why am I even here? This is torture! I can't do this."

"You have to, cousin. You need to be here, but..."

"But what?"

"Shanell, I know you're not gonna want to hear this, but you need to tell him about the babies."

"I can't! Not yet."

"How do you expect to keep this from him? I can see a change in you already. You don't think he's going to notice?"

"I think you're only seeing it because you know about it. No one else has said a word."

"What about doctor's appointments? You know Marcus and Evan are going to be glued to you now."

I shook my head. I knew I didn't have all the answers yet, but telling him wasn't one of them.

"I don't know. I haven't thought about all of that."

"Well, Shanell, you need to. They're gonna know from that alone, and they might end up telling Jay."

I knew she was right, but I had to think of something to throw them off since telling anyone else was not an option.

"Nevaeh, I'm gonna need you as my cover again."

"What?"

"Just for a little while. You're not going back to work any time soon, right?"

"No, but Shanell, I have things at home that I still need to take care of."

"Please! I just need a few more weeks. Until I don't have to stay here anymore."

"And then what are you gonna do?"

"I don't know, but we fooled Marcus before into thinking the consultations were for you. I know we can do it again. I just have to come up with a really good plan."

She stood up, angry.

"Are you serious, Shanell!"

Ms. Janine and my mom came up the stairs and in the room.

"Oh, so there you two are." My mom noticed how tense Nevaeh was once they entered the room along with her sudden movement in facing them. "Baby, are you two okay?"

"Yeah, Mom. I'm fine."

"Nevaeh?" she asked.

"I'm fine too, Auntie. We were just talking, and I needed to stretch." Then Jay came in the room too.

"I see the party been moved up here."

And yet you get to attend another one later tonight. How happy are you?

"What were you doing?" his mom asked.

"I was down in the theater listening to music. I got a call from Geo asking me if I was up to working on a video for 'Loving You'." His mom was happy to hear that.

"Oh, Jay, that's great! So do you think you're ready to get back in the swing of things?"

I kindly answered that.

"Oh yeah, he's ready."

Jay just stared at me, not amused. He knew that was a jab at him.

"Would y'all mind if I spoke to my *fiancée* for a second?"

"We wouldn't have it any other way," said my mom. She put her hands on Nevaeh's shoulders, walking behind her as she left out. His mom smiled at me and then shut the door, since she was last to leave us. Jay came and sat beside me on the bed.

"Look, I'm sorry about earlier. I didn't mean no disrespect to you, and I promise from here on out you won't hafta worry about anything like that happening again."

I remained silent for a minute and just stared at the floor. I could feel Jay's eyes staring at me, waiting for a response. I finally looked at him.

"Okay. Apology accepted."

"Thank you!"

"So, you're about to do a video for 'Loving You'?"

"Yeah, so I won't be here, but Marcus and E are usually with you, right?"

"Yup! I'll be fine. I'll be busy anyway with therapy and doctor's visits... uh... I meant visits here from the nurse."

"Yeah... okay. I had to get a new phone, so I'mma leave you the number before I go."

"You're leaving already?"

"Have to. I gotta learn the song all over again, so I'mma be with Kyle. It's time I got back on my grind anyway. Plus, I needa get familiar with being back in the studio."

"Will I see you later then?"

"I should be back here tonight." My attention shifted back down to the floor again. "You okay? We good?"

I paused and stared in his handsome face that was blowing me right now before I responded. As much as I felt like I couldn't be here, knowing that he wouldn't, scared me even more. I wasn't okay, and no we weren't good! I wanted to scream out, 'Remember me, damnit! I love you!' And because of that love, I lied.

"Yeah, we're good."

He gave me a hug and, in the process, tried to bring my body over so I would've been flat on him. I knew I couldn't be on my stomach really, so I panicked and pushed him away.

"Jay, get off me!" He was shook by my reaction. I'm sure it was because I said things were good, yet I hollered at him. I got up to create a little space.

Jay

Her words echoed in my head. I had another flashback.

"Jay, what is it?"

I couldn't take my eyes off her face as she looked down at me.

"You said that to me before, with that same tone in ya voice. You pushed me away then too. Why?"

Shanell had the biggest smile on her face.

"Something came to you again. Baby, I'm so happy right now!" Then she sat back beside me. "But I need you to give me a little more." I was trying real hard to focus on the glimpse that just flashed in my head from her words.

"I just remembered grabbing you and us sitting on a bed just like this, but you kept pushing me away."

"Jay, the moment I think you're talking about was when I had just found out that you had slept with Nikki and she was carrying your baby."

"So how many times I done slept with this girl?"

"It better had been only once, which was when she won the contest to have dinner with you. I was upset about hearing that you had sex with her because I had heard it from her and not you. Although, in your defense, she drugged you."

"Hold up! So you heard she drugged me too?"

"Yeah! Jay you told me. She did drug you. Ask Spence about it. He'll tell you. Nikki put something in your water, took you up in one of the rooms, and got you to have sex with her. You were trying to get me to listen to you and hear you out at that particular time." Right then, I really started having my doubts about Nikki. Too many people were saying the same shit, and here I was, tryna give her the benefit of the doubt. I came to the realization that Nikki had been lying to me, and she was not the type of person I thought she was. Shanell put her hand on my shoulder, which broke my concentration.

"Are you remembering something else?"

"Nah, just thinking 'bout a few things. I'mma get outta here. I'll leave the number down in the office." I stood to my feet. "You going back downstairs?"

"Yeah."

I took Shanell's hand and helped her up off the bed. Then we both went downstairs with the others. Everyone was in the family room. At the same time, we both noticed Lyric was now here.

"Hey, Jay bear!"

She gave me a hug and then she spoke to Shanell, hugging her as well.

"Well I'm 'bout to head out, everybody."

Lyric squinted her eyes, baffled.

"Why are you leaving? I just got here?"

"I gotta get up with Kyle. 'Bouta do the video for 'Loving You', so I gotta learn the song."

"Ooo that's my shhii—song." She had to catch herself. "Well, now that Shanell's home, Jay, we need to all go out and celebrate. When you gon' be ready," she asked while smacking her hands repeatedly behind her.

"I'm ready whenever she is."

Everyone looked at Shanell, especially her mom and Nevaeh. They were really interested in her response.

"I guess I wouldn't mind going out for that occasion."

"Well it's settled. Jay, when you get done handling ya business, we're all going out."

"I'm cool with that. Alright! Lemme get outta here."

Nevaeh called my name.

"Uh, Jay. Can I have a chat with you before you leave? I promise it'll be fast."

"Yeah, sure! Let me say my goodbyes real quick, and you can walk me out and talk."

I gave everyone hugs goodbye before we headed out front.

"Look, I know this is none of my business, but how dare you do that to my cousin when she's just coming home."

"I apologized to Shanell about it, and you right. I shouldn't have taken the call at that time. I can admit I was wrong for that."

"I really hope you mean that. She's been through a lot, well you both have. I know you don't remember things too well yet, but I always stick up for you, Jay, because I know you mean well when it comes to her. But I also call it like I see it. Shanell doesn't need more added stress, so since you want her here, it's up to you to make sure that happens. If you're not going to see to that, it's no need for her to be here, and I will see to it that she leaves. We clear?"

"Look, I know that's ya cousin, and I can respect ya position... believe me I'mma look out for her, alright?"

"Okay. That's all I ask."

"Can I go now? You not gon' hit me when I turn my back are you?"

She playfully pushed me away.

"Get outta here! We're done."

Shanell

Spence went out the door once he saw Nevaeh had come in. She joined Lyric and me down in the theater. We were having some girl talk while my mom and Ms. Murphy continued to talk upstairs. I just had to be nosy.

"What was that all about?"

"I believe I asked Jay to talk," she recalled.

"Well excuse me."

"Yes, mind ya business."

My mouth hung open, leaving me looking stupid. Then I smacked my lips and rolled my eyes at Nevaeh and just let her have that. Lyric filled her in on what we were discussing, which was Jay.

"You ladies good?"

Every so often, Marcus would make an appearance to check on me. Nevaeh looked over by the door where Marcus was standing.

"Don't worry. Shanell's not going anywhere."

He shook his head and smiled.

"You damn right she ain't, and just so we're clear, I'm still coming back to check on her again." He turned around and left. When I glanced over at Nevaeh, she was still staring at the doorway, smiling. I snapped my fingers at her.

"What," she said innocently.

"You know what," stated Lyric. "You feelin' him?" She started snapping her fingers and teasing her in song. "You feelin' him... you feelin', you feelin', you feelin', you feelin' him." I was cracking up, but Nevaeh didn't laugh.

"No, girl! So stop with that singing."

"Girl, Marcus is sexy," Lyric expressed.

"Can we talk about someone else, please?" Nevaeh begged while rolling her eyes.

I figured I'd come to her rescue. Neveah didn't openly express her feelings much, unless she really felt comfortable, so I knew she wouldn't admit anything about Marcus in front of Lyric. But I could tell something was brewing inside her.

"Okay, fine! Lyric, how's your boo doing?"

We talked in the theater a little while longer, and then eventually we all went back upstairs, and I spent some time talking to my mom in private.

"Shanell, I really think you should tell Jay about the pregnancy. Baby, I can't stress this enough that I think you're making a big mistake."

There was nothing she could say to make me change my mind on this. I was going to handle it how I saw fit.

"Mom, please just respect my wishes. I know you don't agree with them, but I'm not budging on this."

"Okay. It's your life, so I'll have to respect your decision. Anyway, I'll be going back home soon. You know I have to get back to work so I can be able to take some time off when my grandbabies are born." That made me think about when I was fussing with Jay in the hospital about not coming home with him. He said that I didn't know how much longer my mom and Nevaeh would be here in town, when I was so sure they would be staying for a while. I started laughing at myself. I hated that he was right. My mom looked at me like I was crazy. She probably thought I was losing it. "Why are you laughing?"

"Mom, please don't pay me any mind right now. It's nothing." Once our talk was over, we rejoined everyone else who was congregating in the kitchen. Time went by, and we all ate dinner. Before it had gotten too late, Mom, Nevaeh, and Lyric were saying their goodbyes. I went in the office and saw the number Jay left for me. He always had the nicest handwriting. Right below it, the words 'I'm sorry' were there. I smiled. I wondered if this nightmare was ever going to be over.

Jay

I met up with Kyle to get familiar with being in the studio and to go over the song that day. It didn't take me long to learn it. That next day, I found out that I would be going to *Fallchester City* soon to shoot the video. When I told Shanell, she had mixed feelings about it. We were in the kitchen discussing it.

"Jay, I know you still have to work, but are you sure you're ready to do this? That's a big place like here. Your fanbase is just as large there, and no one knows about your amnesia. Are you going to be able to handle the paparazzi and all you may encounter so soon?"

"I'm sure I'll be fine. Besides, I'm ready. I needa do this, you know?"

"Yeah... I guess."

Shanell left out the room looking upset. I went to grab a drink from the fridge when Lyric came in there.

"What you do to Shanell now?"

She sat down at the round table.

"I ain't do nothing to her. I think she mad because I gotta go out of town so soon."

"Where you going now?"

"Do a video shoot in *Fallchester City*."

"I'm coming too then. I know you're going to be working, but I figure I can get some shopping done for my business, and when you're not working, we could hang out."

"I don't know, Lyric. Don't you needa be discussing this with ya man first?"

"Don't worry about my relationship. You just focus on yours, okay?"

I laughed.

"Whatever, man."

Shanell

As much as I wasn't happy about Jay leaving, the only good thing about it, at least, was that it gave me more time to figure out how I could continue to hide this pregnancy from him. My mom stayed for another week before she left on a Friday morning to go back home. She wanted to make sure I was settling in and my vitals were all good. She made me promise to call her to keep her updated on everything and not to stress about Jay being gone when he finally left.

That day was here. He left the following Monday after my mom left. The only reason I didn't stress about it was because

I knew Lyric would be traveling with him. I knew she'd keep a bitch in line, watch Jay's behavior, and check him if necessary. That was the only thing keeping me sane. I did my usual routine and made sure he had everything packed that he was going to need. His team was waiting for him out in the car. I walked him to the door, gave him a gentle kiss, and then said three words that I meant with every fiber of my being.

"I love you." Jay was about to respond, but I covered his lips. "Just have a safe flight, and call me when you get there." I moved my finger away.

"But you don't even know what I was about to say."

"I know you love me. I'm just waiting to hear it from you when you really remember how much you love me."

Jay left it at that and walked out the door to go to the car.

Chapter Eight

THIRSTY BITCHES

J ay

$\mathbf{1^{st}}$ *day on set*

The concept of the "Loving You" video was fairly simple. They didn't want to have too much going on since they wanted to gradually bring me back to work. They shot the video in one location to keep it less complicated. They told me it would be done like I was at a party with my girl. We'd be mingling and having a good time with friends, which was something I was already familiar with. I really didn't have too much to do but enjoy being with her and singing to her, showing her what it meant to me to love her.

I was still waiting to meet my leading lady and for a few more of the extras to be done with make up before they got started. In the meantime, I was talking to the director, Zharvis Gregory, when a young lady walked up.

"Jay, you remember Dream."

"Hey," she said then flashed an amazing smile. "I'm so glad to see you're back up on your feet again. I tried to get in touch with you to see how you were but never got a response."

"Oh... yeah... I end up gettin' a new phone."

Her wild, curly hair complimented her round face.

"If you two will excuse me. I'll let you know when we'll be ready to begin." Zharvis left us there to continue talking. She nodded her head at me and smiled.

"You look great, Jay." She bit the corner of her lip ever so slightly. Shit looked seductive. "You look very distinguished without your braids. Very sexy!"

I had no clue who Dream was, but she obviously knew me. She was real easy on the eyes, and she thought *I* was sexy? I halfway smiled.

"Thanks for the compliment."

"Who knew I'd be your leading lady again, right? Although we did nail the last video we did together. We made love look so real, people actually thought we were seeing each other."

So that's how we know each other. Suddenly, someone tapped me on my shoulder from behind. When I turned around, it was Autumn. My eyes grew from surprise.

"Aye, girl! What you doing here?"

"I'll let you two talk, Jay. See you in a bit."

"Alright, baby." She smiled at Autumn too before she walked off. "So what you doing here?" I asked as I hugged her.

I'm an extra in the video. I was trying to get the leading lady role. How come you didn't pick me?"

She had me laughing.

"Nah, it wasn't like that at all. I don't even choose."

"Sure! Now my feelings are hurt," she claimed as she folded her arms and playfully looked away from me.

"Aw, love, I can't have that. What can I do to fix it?"

"Well, dinner would be nice."

"Oh, you tryna make a nigga spend money." She blared her beautiful exotic eyes at me.

"I'll pay for it. I just really want your company," she said as she spruced up my collar on my shirt.

"How 'bout we just have a drink while we here? I can't really say what I'm doing later to schedule a dinner with you."

"I'll take it."

We were interrupted since it was time to get things started. The director went over what we were going to be shooting first and instructed me on what I needed to do. We worked on the video into the wee hours of the morning, since we started shooting at night. Autumn and I never did get to have drinks that day; it was just too much on me.

The next day before I had to be back on the set, Lyric wanted me to go out with her while she got some shopping done. I did want to spend some time with her, so I went. I picked up a few pairs of sneaks, some more shades, and a new watch.

Then I was ready to go, but not Lyric. She got her some jewelry, two pairs of shoes, one pair of boots, and some lingerie.

"I thought you were shopping for ya business."

"This is business. I have to look good while I'm handling my business."

I just laughed at her crazy ass. We were out at the stores for a few hours, mostly because Spence was tryna keep me from getting mobbed in these streets. It had been crazy out here. Shanell was right, but I'd been holding my own. Finally, we were going to stop somewhere to get something to eat. While we were riding in the car, my phone rang.

"What's up?"

"What are you doing?"

"'Bouta go eat."

"Where at?"

"I don't know yet. We still tryna decide."

"Do you mind if I join you guys?"

"Nah."

"So where are y'all gonna go?"

"I'mma text you with that info as soon I find out, alright?"

"Okay. I'll see you soon." I hung up. Lyric was eyeing me throughout the whole conversation.

"Who was that?"

"That was just Autumn."

"Who the hell is she?"

"Why you snappin'? She cool."

"She's coming?"

"Yeah! Why?"

"How you know I didn't want to spend time with you alone? Why'd you invite

her?"

"I didn't. She asked me if she could come."

"Don't you have a woman who's waiting for you at home that you should *only* be eating with for pleasure?"

I started laughing at her crazy ass.

"What, you my chaperone now? I ain't doing nothing. We only eating."

"She can eat by her damn self. What she needs to eat with you for?"

"Look, it ain't even that serious. I told you she cool."

"She ain't cool if she knows about Shanell and still tryna be up in ya face, but aye, I'm just a female who's been around you for years and don't know anything about thirsty bitches."

Everyone in the car laughed. Even I had to laugh on that comment. Even though I was still getting to know Lyric, she continued to amaze me with her dominant personality and the things that she would say. Once we decided on where to go, I texted Autumn with the info. When we arrived and were about to be seated, my phone started going off again.

"Y'all go 'head. I needa take this."

This time it was Nikki. I started not to answer it, but I did in case it was something about the baby.

"Aye!"

"Hey, boo! What you doing?"

"I'm getting something to eat right now. Something wrong?"

"No, I just wanted to hear your voice. I miss you. I wanted to know when I was going to see you again, besides the doctor's visits. We haven't spoken since the last time you said you'd call me back."

"I can't answer that right now, because I'm out of town."

"Where you at?"

"In *Fallchester*, working."

"How long you going to be there?"

"Until I get done."

"Jay, I wanna see you."

"Look, I'm 'bouta eat right now, so I'mma call you when I get some more free time."

"You said that before and you never did it—Ow!"

"What happened? What's wrong?"

Nikki

"I just felt a sharp pain or something in my stomach."

"Is this the first time that's happened?"

"Yeah, and I hope it's the last."

Listening to his concern had me so hopeful that he would come see me.

"Are you home?" *Hmm... if I say yes that may make him less paranoid.*

"No, I'm out with Charmaine."

"Where y'all going?"

"To a party."

I heard him heavily sigh on the other end.

"So you still going out, huh?"

"I can't just sit in the house, Jay, unless I'm spending time with yo—Oww!"

"It happened again?"

"Yes! I need to... to sit."

I was standing straight up in my house alone.

"Where Charmaine? Is she near you?"

"Jay, I gotta go." I hung up. "Hahaha!" I noticed him calling me back, but I just let it ring. He called again, but I wasn't picking up. "That'll make you think about me while you're gone, negro."

I sat back on my couch and continued watching TV.

Jay

"Fuck!"

It looked like I scared a few people from my sudden outburst, but I didn't care. She had me thinking all kinds of shit once she hung up. I wanted to know what the fuck happened and if she was alright. I tried to find comfort in knowing that she wasn't alone, since she was with Charmaine, but it bothered me that she wasn't answering.

I walked over to the table and joined the others. Autumn had arrived shortly after and was surprised when she saw an unfamiliar face at the table. I introduced her to Lyric since they had never met. Autumn didn't look too pleased when she was introduced either. I could see a hint of jealousy that showed since I never introduced Lyric as my best friend. She likely thought Lyric was another groupie that beat her to the punch, I'm sure.

We placed our orders, and finally the food was brought over to the table. Lyric pretty much was taking over the conversation.

"How was the video shoot, Jay bear?"

Autumn politely gave her input.

"It was so fun!" she gushed. "Wasn't it, Jay?" Lyric looked at her with an evil grimace for butting in. "Jay was dressed so handsome as he played his part," she said, putting her hand on my shoulder. "We even got to interact for a second." Lyric narrowed her eyes at me, and her mouth opened a peek.

"Hmm, it's funny because I don't remember asking you. I said Jay, and I know for a fact that's not your name. *Jay!*" she stressed, looking back at me. "Jay! You okay?"

"I'm sorry. My mind was elsewhere. Can y'all excuse me for a second?" I walked over to the lounge where it was less chatter and tried calling Nikki again. This time she answered. "Yo! What's goin' on? You okay? E'rything alright with the baby?"

"Hey, baby! You actually called me back."

"Fuck you talkin' bout? I been tryna call you. You can't see that I called?"

"Baby, I'm sorry. My phone has been on the charger. It died when we got disconnected." I shook my head in frustration.

"Are you alright?"

"Yeah, I'm fine. Why?"

"Why? I thought ya stomach was bothering you?"

"Oh... that was nothing. I think it was gas pains."

I couldn't believe it. I was so irritated with her right now. "We gon' talk when I get back, alright?"

"I'm looking forward to it."

"Alright. I'll talk to you later."

"You hanging up with me already?"

"Yeah, I gotta get back to work."

"Okay. I love you."

"Yeah, alright."

I was relieved that it was nothing wrong for the most part but upset because she scared me, and I didn't know what was going on. That prompted me to call Shanell. I just needed to hear her voice for some reason.

"Hello."

"Aye."

"Hey!" She had so much joy in that one word. It made me smile automatically. "How's the video going?"

"It's goin' good. I'm 'bout to go back on the set pretty soon. I just was calling to check on you."

"I'm just sitting up here in the office checking some emails. I got so much work to do. I'm so glad my boss loves me. If I was working somewhere else, they probably would've fired me by now."

"I never even found out what you did for a living."

"I work for *Lit Magazine* in Public Relations. I've even interviewed you before."

"That's right! Somebody did tell me that. How'd I do?"

"You did very well, as you do with all your interviews."

"You gon' hafta show me that one. You still have it?"

"Jay, I have every interview that you've done since we've been together."

"Seriously?"

"Okay, *you* have them, but they might as well be mine since I watch them more than you."

I found myself smiling with her, and it felt good.

"You be going back and watching 'em?"

"Yeah. I like to get pointers from other journalists who's been in the business longer than me. Plus, they're usually talking about my favorite topic."

"What's that?"

"You."

Damn! That had me blushing like a bitch.

"Who's there with you?"

"Marcus and Evan are here, which reminds me, Jay, why is that? Evan is usually with me at night, only."

"I made a few adjustments. Don't worry. E'rything alright. How you doing with ya therapy?"

"Oh my God! It's exhausting! My body be so tired afterwards. I always fall asleep."

I couldn't stop grinning.

"Has the visiting nurse came yet?"

"No. I don't see her until Friday."

"Oh, alright. You gon' call me and tell me how everything went?"

"Sure!"

"Cool! Well I'm 'bouta head back to the set. I'mma probably call you again later on tonight. It's gon' be late doe."

"For you, maybe. Don't forget about the time difference here."

"Damn! I did forget."

"Okay, baby, that's fine, and if you can't I'll understand that too, but I am glad you had a moment to call me. Go 'head and do what you gotta do, and hopefully we'll talk later."

I felt real good after talking to Shanell. She was just what I needed. I was now relaxed and in a better mood. When I came back to the table, I was like a different person. Everyone noticed it.

"Y'all ready?"

Lyric looked at my plate, which was barely touched.

"You're not gonna finish your food?"

"Nah, I'm good." I looked at my watch. "We needa go." Then Autumn jumped in.

"Jay, we still have an hour and a half before we have to be there."

"I know, but I got a few things to do first before I go back. I'mma go and get this bill paid, and then we gon' be out."

I went to take care of the tab. Autumn followed right behind me. As soon as Lyric saw her get up, she followed behind her. Shortly after, everybody just got up from the table and was headed over by the exit. The driver was outside waiting by the time we settled the bill. Everyone else went on and got in the truck. Spence went with me to walk Autumn to her car, which had been brought up by valet. I saw Lyric start to follow us over to Autumn's car acting like she wanted to see her off too, but she turned around and got in the truck.

"I'll be waiting, Jay!" Lyric yelled. "Bye, Autumn!"

Autumn frowned her face at her. She didn't like that one bit.

"Who does she think she is? How do you know her?"

"That's not important, honestly."

Lyric wasn't done and was still talking shit. She poked her head out the window.

"Come on, Jay bear! We gotta get back to the room so you can finish looking at my goods." Spence and I both looked at Lyric with half smiles on our faces. We knew what she was doing, and it was working because Autumn was all in her feelings. I didn't pay Lyric any mind since I was starting to understand her personality, but Autumn didn't, and as far as I was concerned, she didn't have to. Lyric wasn't her business.

"Really, Jay! What's with her?"

"She don't mean no harm. Just get in the car." I opened the door for her. "Alright, drive safe, and I'll see you in a bit."

"She won't be on set, right?"

"No."

"Good! I'll see you soon."

"Later, baby."

As soon as I got in the car, Lyric started her shit about Autumn.

"I only have one thing to say about her, and then you won't hear me talk about her again."

"Do I really wanna know?"

"I don't care if you don't, but that bitch dry as the desert and fiending for you to quench her thirst, but I'mma solve all that and put my fist down her damn throat. That'll do it. There I'm done."

"You sure?"

"Yes! Now I'm about to call my baby because I see I done missed his call."

She spent the whole car ride on the phone with her man and still was talking to him once we reached the *Regal Roy El Hotel*. I got on the computer to do some research real quick on DNA testing and the dangers during pregnancy. I really needed to know the risk before I brought it up to Nikki again.

Then I got in the shower and got myself ready to get back to the set. I had to admit that I was really enjoying the process so far for doing this video. I was thinking about talking to Kyle about tackling a few new songs.

Lyric

I was on the phone with Shanell while I was lying on the bed in the hotel room. It had been a full two weeks since we had been in *Fallchester City*. I had been trying to get Shanell to come here when I found out from Jay that this Saturday night, they were having a wrap up party, for the completion of the video.

"Shanell, girl, are you coming?"

"I don't know, Lyric. Jay didn't even tell me about it, so maybe I shouldn't."

"Girl, if you don't come on. I want you here. I told you to come and bring Nevaeh with you. Come on! We gon' have some fun."

"You know I don't really do the party scene too much."

"What did I tell you? We need to celebrate, and this would be perfect! You've been cooped up in that hospital and now that house. You need to get out. It's only for a night, or the weekend rather. Please, Shanell?"

"Okay! And I already talked to Nevaeh. She said she was down if I wanted to go, so I'll let her know we're going."

"Yay! You watch. We're going to have so much fun. Plus, I think you being here is gonna be good for Jay. He misses you."

"How you know?"

"I just know. Get ya ass on the earliest flight, and get here ASAP!"

"My flight actually leaves tonight."

"Heifer, you had me do all this begging when you knew you were coming all along?"

"I love you too Lyric."

Shanell

Me and Nevaeh finally made it to the *Regal Roy El* in *Fallchester City*. Evan and Marcus of course were with us. It was around 5:00 am Saturday morning when we got in. I was exhausted. I slept until I couldn't lay no more. I noticed Nevaeh's bed was empty, and it was quiet throughout the suite. She knew I needed my rest. My sleep was broken several times from going to the bathroom. I was just sitting up on the bed stretching when I heard the door open. I figured it must be Nevaeh, since she was gone, but I saw Lyric first.

"I was about to come and wake ya ass up!"

"What time is it?"

"Time for you to get up," she snapped, smacking the bed several times. "We got things to do."

I was sitting up when they came in but then I fell back on the bed, wrapping the blanket over me. I covered my mouth as I yawned.

"I am so restless."

"We can tell. We were going to grab some lunch. Get up and get dressed."

"Y'all might have to go without me."

"For what!"

"Lyric, it's going to take me another hour just to be fully awake. Then I gotta get dressed. I don't wanna be holding y'all up."

"So don't! Come on! Get ya butt up and get dressed now so we can eat."

Nevaeh walked in. I squirmed around, loving the lavishness of the bed.

"This bed is so comfortable. I feel right at home."

Nevaeh crossed her arms and sighed.

"I get it, but are you coming with us or not!"

"Alright already. I'm getting up. Just give me ten more minutes."

Lyric clapped her hands at me, startling me.

"Ten minutes! Come on, Nevaeh. Shanell, we'll be down in the lounge. Hurry up!"

"I'll be there. Lyric, where's Jay?"

"He went somewhere with Kyle."

"I didn't know Kyle was in town too. Does he know I'm here?"

"No, but so what? I think it's going to be a nice surprise when he sees you here tonight."

Nevaeh peered at Lyric.

"What about Evan and Marcus? Do you think he's spoken to either one of them to know she's here?"

"Well, if he knows, he knows. Shit! She should be here more than anybody."

"Anybody like who? Who else is here?" I wondered.

"That Autumn chick is here, but only because she was in the video too."

Hearing that got my adrenaline pumping.

"He's been around her these past two weeks?"

"Oh, believe me, ain't nothing go down with her... trust!" That gave me all the energy I needed. I sat up in that bed real quick.

"I'll be ready shortly. Y'all are going to be in the lounge, right?"

"Yeah, and then we're eating in *The Hot Lodge Cafe* here in the hotel, okay?"

"Okay."

Nevaeh

As soon as Lyric and I opened the door, Evan and Marcus were standing right there. Lyric said hello first.

"What's up, fellas?"

"Shanell still in there?"

"Yes, Marcus. Shouldn't you know that?" I asked, staring at him sideways.

"Why you always gotta give me a hard time?"

"You can handle it." Evan broke up our back and forth. "Where're you two off too?"

"We're waiting for Miss Slowpoke to get ready so we can have brunch, but for now we're about to go in the café," Lyric told him.

"We were just coming to find out what was on her agenda for today before this one started busting my balls."

I really wanted to say something to Marcus about his balls, but Lyric told him what he wanted to know.

"Well, after we eat, we're going to the spa, and then we'll be getting ready for the party tonight."

"I can't wait to get my back worked on," I said as I put both hands on my hips

trying to stretch my spine. Marcus looked at me with one eyebrow raised.

"I can do it for you." Then he held up his hands. "These hands are lethal." Lyric started giggling and Evan just shook his head.

"How 'bout you keep your lethal weapons over there?" I insisted, shoving his hands away. "I'm not ready to die yet."

"I bet you'd die smiling," he bragged. I did just that and

smiled. I couldn't even say anything, which was a first. "So she in the room getting dressed?"

"Yes, Sherlock!" Evan looked at us both.

"Alright. We'll be down with her once she gets ready."

"Okay," Lyric said in a serious tone, mocking Evan before we headed down to the cafe. We noticed it was raining out. "I hope it doesn't stay like this for the rest of the day."

"I know. This weather fucks with my back. I hate it."

"I hate having normal back aches. I couldn't imagine one from an injury."

We finally entered the cafe. There were a few people sitting in there talking. They didn't start serving drinks until 2:30, so nothing was open yet. Nevaeh and I went to take a seat over by the fireplace. It was beautiful. The face of it was so long it covered most of the wall it was a part of. We wanted to melt in those seats once we sat in them. They were so comfortable. It made me think about Shanell.

"We can't let Shanell sit down once she gets here."

"Why not?"

"She's not gonna want to get up."

We both started cracking up.

"I wish she would hurry up. I'm starving."

Shortly after, Shanell, Evan, and Marcus all walked up.

"I heard y'all laughing way over there. I'm here already."

"Well, it took you long enough," Lyric told her. "The party's not until tonight. I see you took extra time to look good in case you bumped into your boo?" Lyric was joking with her.

"Be quiet!"

We went to be seated and prepared to have lunch. We stayed in there, talked, and joked around with one another for a good two hours. We still had the spa to go to. I had to mess with Marcus about it since he had to accompany Shanell.

"So, Marcus, are you getting worked on in the spa? You seem a bit uptight."

He lifted his head back some.

"Are you gonna do it?"

"I guess that's a no."

Lyric was just staring at Evan with this puzzling look on her face.

"Evan, why you never talk? You're always so quiet and serious."

"I talk."

I joined in. "Not as much as this one," I joked, looking at Marcus.

"... You want me, don't you?" Then he flexed his muscles. We all screamed. Since we were sitting by each other, he grabbed my shoulders, letting me know he was just playing. My body said hello the minute he laid hands on me. Evan started defending himself to Lyric.

"Marcus know I have my moments. I just be focused on the task at hand."

"Okay, but you need to relax sometimes and laugh."

He laughed.

"Now we're talking," said Lyric.

Shanell got up.

"I'm going to stop at the bathroom and then we can head to the spa guys."

Once Shanell was back, we got up from the table and went to get our spa treatments. Evan and Marcus had a seat in the waiting area.

Chapter Nine

REMEMBER ME

S *hanell*

"Now, Shanell, just to let you know when you go back there, we will be accompanying you to see what room you're in and who's your masseuse."

"Marcus, that's fine, but know once you see that, you're going back in the front."

"Believe me, we know."

Lyric was up at the desk, letting them know that we were here for our appointments. She scheduled us all for regular massages. The receptionist told us to have a seat. We did even though Lyric was still there asking questions. I was looking over everything they had to offer. Something caught my eye.

"Ooo! Nevaeh look, they have one for a mother-to-be." Evan and Marcus curiously looked at me, wondering why I got excited about that. I could tell Nevaeh didn't know how to react. I had to think fast. "I just think that's cool that they offer something like that for pregnant women, okay, so stop looking at me like I said something crazy."

"Well alright then," Lyric replied. "Now that that's settled, everybody stop looking at the girl like she said something crazy!"

I was cracking up. She had no idea why I said that because she was just coming back from the front desk. She just heard me as she walked up and repeated me. It was finally time for us to be seen. Evan and Marcus went in the back and briefly spoke to my masseuse, and then they walked back out front to have a seat. My masseuse's name was Cindy.

"Hey, Cindy, is it too late to change my choice to the Mother-to-be massage? I'm carrying twins, and I didn't want to ask for that in front of everyone."

"Sure! It's not too late at all. It would impact the price only, if that was okay."

"No problem!"

"Congratulations!"

"Thank you!"

"That has to be exciting, right?"

"A little scary as well, but I'm excited too."

She suddenly covered her mouth as she looked at me.

"Oh my gosh! I know who you are. You're engaged to Jay Murphy, aren't you?"

With hesitance, I answered her.

"Uh... yeah... that's me."

"I'm going to take real good care of you. I love his music!

Oh my gosh!" she blurted. "This is so unbelievable! You guys are having twins!"

"Can you please keep your voice down." *I don't know what I was thinking... this is such a bad idea.*

"I'm sorry! My lips are sealed. I'll let you get ready and be right back."

Our massages were eighty minutes long. Once I came out, I was floating on air. We all had the sleepy look. Our bodies were feeling good. I looked at them both.

"Oh, I needed that. Now I need a nap."

"No! I needed that," challenged Nevaeh. "I'm ready to pack Joy up with me."

"I had Mary," said Lyric. "She was the bomb too."

Marcus carefully eyed all of us.

"Y'all look like y'all was spending ya energy doing something else back there... walking all slow."

Nevaeh had to respond.

"You jealous?"

"No, ma'am."

"Everyone is pleased. Y'all feeling good now?" asked Evan.

"Evan, it was the best. You should make an appointment," Lyric told him. He laughed. "I'm about to go to sleep."

"Me too, so Evan, Marcus, that's where I'll be, in my room taking a nap. Y'all know the party's at 11:00 pm, right?" I confirmed.

"Yes," answered Evan. "We're still gonna walk with you up to the room, and then I'll come check on you later to see when you wanna leave."

Lyric

We all went to our rooms to get some sleep for a while. I was awakened by knocking on the door. They banged so hard you would have thought it was the police. I looked through the peephole, and it was Jay. I could've killed him.

"What were you doing?"

"Sleep!"

"Wake ya ass up! Sleep's overrated."

"Boy, leave me alone," I growled as I rolled my eyes at him, walked back over to the bed, and snuggled back underneath the covers. "What you do most of the day?"

"Hang out. Nothing to really talk about. You still going to the party?"

"Of course!"

I couldn't wait to see his expression when he saw Shanell if he didn't know already that she was here. Jay finally sat down in the chair close by the window.

"Whatchu been doing today? Why you so sleepy?"

"I had the best massage ever."

"From where?"

"A spot here in the hotel. That shit felt so good, you just don't know. I didn't want to get off that table."

"It must was good. You barely wanted to get out the bed."

I was curious to know if he knew Shanell was here.

"You should do that for Shanell one day."

"Yeah, something like that would be nice, especially since

she's been in the hospital for the longest. I probably do it for her some time when I get back home. Who knows?"

Bingo! I got what I was looking for. We continued to talk about the past week's events and the party tonight.

"So what's the deal with Autumn? Why do you even entertain her?"

"She's just a real cool girl that I may holla at from time to time."

"Then what are your thoughts concerning you and Shanell?"

He told me about the flashbacks that he had. He never told me things were coming back to him.

"It's the strangest thing to have a memory attached to a feeling, and then just like that, it's gone. It's hard to explain, but in those instances, I knew who she was. There were strong feelings there. All I can say is that I hope I can get that back, but I don't wanna risk hurting her if nothing changes. I'm still confused about a lot of things, and Nikki is one of them.

"Jay, please don't tell me you have feelings for her?"

"No! It's nothing like that. I just don't understand why I been cheating on Shanell with Nikki if I'm so in love with Shanell."

"Jay, you didn't cheat on her. You slept with Nikki one time, and that only happened because she drugged you. You have always been faithful to Shanell, and if Nikki is telling you otherwise, she's lying. You wouldn't give her the time of day, and she hated that."

"What about Autumn?"

"What about her?"

"I don't know if I had sex with her, but I kissed her."

"When?"

"She told me it happened after one of my shows while Shanell was in the hospital."

"You were cheating on her while she was in a coma?"

"That's what I'm saying. I don't know. Autumn just told me she kissed me. She did say she took advantage of the situation. I guess I would talk to her about Shanell, but..."

"Yeah, and that bitch just had to be there. I *really* don't like her now."

"Do you even have many people that you like?" I threw a pillow at him. He caught it. "Yo' ass just mean."

"I'm not mean!"

"You one of them mean ass pretty girls."

"Well if I am, you love it."

"Yeah, so you and my momma tell me. Alright, I'm 'bouta go get in the shower and start getting ready. We probably leave like eleven thirty-ish."

"Oh, you guys go ahead. I gotta make a stop first, and then I'll be there."

"Who gon' be with you?"

"Nobody. Why?"

"'Cause you shouldn't be traveling alone like that. I'mma get one of them cats to stay with you."

"No, Jay, you don't have to do that. I'll be fine. I promise you."

"Nah, I'm really not comfortable with that, Lyric."

"Okay, fine! I won't be by myself so don't worry."

"Who you gon' be with?"

"A guy that I know very well."

"Yeah, that's probably who you were with earlier today. That's why ya ass so tired."

"Shut up, boy! I ain't cheating on my boo."

"Oh, we got jokes! Alright!"

After I thought about it, I started laughing. I didn't mean it how he took it. I seriously was just talking about me. By no means was I throwing shade on his situation.

"I wasn't even saying it like that, but I mean, if the shoe fits."

"I'm outta here. I'll see you later."

We arrived at the party around midnight. I wanted to make sure we came after Jay had already left. Shanell had to go to the bathroom when we got here, so she didn't stay with Nevaeh and me. She told us to go ahead and mingle if we wanted to. She would be fine since Evan and Marcus were with her, so those three walked off. I wanted to find out where Jay was anyway.

What do you know? He was spotted having a drink with Autumn all up in his face. I looked around for Spence and didn't see him anywhere. We decided to walk over there and break up that little scene before Shanell saw it. When Jay saw me, he was shocked to see Nevaeh here too. He hugged us both.

"So this why you didn't want to come when I did. Good to see you here, Nevaeh."

"I needed a good party to go to," she joked.

"Is Shanell with y'all too?" As soon as he asked, he spotted her in the back with Evan and Marcus. She was looking around, likely trying to find us. "Oh, Autumn, this is Nevaeh, and you've met Lyric. Can you excuse me for a minute?"

"Uh... yeah... sure."

Jay walked off. We both weren't going to stand there and talk to her, so we just left her ass standing there and went to get some drinks. We later saw Spence at a safe distance watching Jay as he headed toward Shanell.

Shanell

My eyes finally met up with Jays. I saw my baby happily coming in my direction. He always looked good in my eyes, even when he was walking around stripped down to his boxers. Jay looked casually comfortable wearing a black tee, denim jeans, pair of Jordans, and a Giuseppe jacket that tied in with his sneaks.

My heart raced as his eyes penetrated right through me. *When is he gonna remember me?* We both were all smiles as our eyes were fixed on each other. When Jay went to embrace me, he held on a little tighter than usual as he kissed me. I didn't want him to feel my stomach since I tried to conceal it by wearing a spaghetti strap babydoll dress, so I hurriedly let him go and spoke.

"Hey!" I could tell he was put off by my aggression in pushing him away, but he didn't say anything. His eyes said it all though.

"Hello, beautiful. What's goin' on?" he said to E and Marcus as they all shook hands and spoke to each other. Then Evan and Marcus left us to have some time alone.

"I'm surprised to see you here. I saw Nevaeh already. Was wonderin' after seeing her if you made the trip."

"Well, I didn't know how you would feel about me being here. I hope it's a good surprise."

"It's all good," he raved as his eyes savored my frame. "I'm glad you came."

"How come you didn't invite me to come then?"

"Honestly, I wasn't even thinking 'bout it. It's just a party. I wouldn't have had you fly here just for that. You still recuperating, you know?"

"Jay, I've been out for a few weeks now. I'm fine."

Jay's eyes continued to travel all over my body. I was hoping it was because he liked what he saw and not because he noticed I picked up weight.

"Damn, baby, you put '*fine*' to shame." He had me blushing, making me feel like a bashful little girl. "You want a drink or something?"

"Oh, no, I'm good."

He took me by the hand and walked me through the crowd and introduced me to different people that he wanted me to meet. I was so flattered that he did that. As time went on, and all the introductions and small talk was had, I was ready for something to drink, but all I noticed were alcoholic beverages. We went to have a seat in two cozy lounge chairs that were some distance from the bar.

"Jay, do they have any juice or bottled water around?"

"Yeah, which one you want?"

"Cranberry juice is good." Jay was looking around for Evan and Marcus until he spotted them. He saw they were occupied talking but not too far away.

"Jay, I'll be fine," I assured trying to put him at ease. "What are you so worried about?"

"Nah, I just didn't wanna leave you alone."

"Why not? You're the celebrity here, not me. I'll be fine."

"I'll still have the guys keeping a lookout on you. I'll be right back."

As soon as Jay left, some girl maneuvered her way in the seat he was in.

"Oo, girl, my feet are killing me. Is anyone sitting here?"

"Well yeah, but I guess you can sit there... since you're in it."

I continued to look straight ahead as I waited for Jay to come back.

"How are you this evening?"

I glanced over at her, surprised she still was talking to me.

"I'm good. How are you?" I asked, being polite.

"I'll be even better once my feet stop hurting. My girlfriend told me not to wear these shoes, but you know how we got to get all cute." I nicely smiled and looked down at her feet as she was taking her shoes off.

"Those are cute!"

"Thanks! I like them too, but my feet are paying like hell."
We both started laughing. "This is a nice party, isn't it?"

"Yes, it really is."

"Your dress is cute too, by the way. I love the babydoll look."

"Thank you."

My eyes started scanning the room, wondering what was taking Jay so long.

"So are you a guest of someone here?"

"Yes, I'm a guest."

"You looked familiar. That's why I asked. I was in the video."

"Oh nice! What did you do in it?"

"Sat around looking cute with a drink in my hand while Jay did his thing. He is so amazing." I halfway moved my cheeks to smile. I didn't like how happy she was getting over my man, but I played nice.

"Yeah, he really is. I can't wait to see it."

"Me either. I hope the scenes they shot of me actually make it in it." She quickly put her shoes back on. "Well I hope you enjoy the rest of your night. I see someone I need to speak with." She hopped up fast and left. I noticed Nevaeh and Lyric making their way over to me. Lyric was talking, being all animated with her finger the moment she approached me.

"Why was that bitch over here? I hope you put her in her place."

"Who?"

I had no clue what she was talking about.

"The one you were just talking to," she confirmed.

"Why would I put her in her place?"

Nevaeh sat in the empty seat with her nose and forehead crinkled, confused.

"What she tell you?"

"Nothing. She just came over here talking to me while she sat for a minute."

"That was Autumn," Lyric announced.

"What!"

I was dumbfounded.

"Yes! You didn't know that?" she asked.

"Hell, no!"

Nevaeh added to the conversation.

"I was wondering why you were talking to her like y'all were cool."

"I know," chimed in Lyric. "We thought y'all were talking woman to woman or something, which was why we didn't make any moves."

I squinted my eyes, staring at back and forth at both of them.

"How would I know who she was when I've never saw her before?"

That sneaky bitch suddenly had me riled up when I knew I couldn't afford to be.

"Cousin, we thought Jay told you."

"No! He never even mentioned that she was here."

Lyric was beside herself now.

"Then what the hell she say to you?"

"I'm still messed up that she came over here like that." I shook my head, irritated. "She really wasn't talking about anything but how her feet were bothering her. Not once did she let on who she was to me. She did mention being in the video though. I never put the two together."

"Her slick ass knew what she was doing," Nevaeh ranted.

"See, that's the crazy shit," said Lyric. "Where that bitch go? She fittin' to get a beat down."

That was right up Nevaeh's alley.

"Right though! She knew who Shanell was. Why come over and talk when she obviously tryna get at your man?" Lyric was looking around the room to see where she was. She had been itching for Autumn to get out of line.

"Why can't I seem to get away from the bullshit?" I fussed.

"Cousin, don't let that girl bring you out of character. I'll beat that bitch ass if she comes near you again."

"Exactly!" agreed Lyric. "I've been tryna behave, but now she got me in my *I don't give a fuck attitude,* and I ain't gon' give zero fucks about whipping her ass in front of all these people when I see her."

"I don't have time nor the energy for this tonight, and as much as I appreciate you guys having my back, I don't wanna see no fights. I knew I shouldn't have did this."

Lyric tried to convince me otherwise.

"Look, you came here to be with Jay. Don't let her spoil

your night. When he comes back over here, just pick up where you guys left off. Don't even tell him she came over to you. He ain't worried about her, Shanell. His face lit up when he saw you were here. He was talking to me and Nevaeh, but as soon as he saw you, it was a wrap. He left us in the wind."

"Yeah, he did, cousin."

"So how'd you guys know that was Autumn?" Nevaeh and Lyric looked at one another, lending no words. "Oh, that's right, Lyric. I forgot you saw her before."

"Right, and I showed her to Nevaeh when I noticed she was here."

Finally, Jay was back with my drink.

"Well, did you have to make the drinks too, Jay," I said sarcastically.

"I'm sorry it took me so long. I was stopped by one of the producers who was talking my ears off. Here you go." He looked at me and smiled. That made my whole mood change.

Nevaeh and Lyric stuck around for a little bit, and all of us were talking for a while. Evan, Marcus, and Spence came over too. Marcus asked Nevaeh if she wanted to dance. She went ahead and danced with him. Lyric grabbed Evan up and made him dance with her. She was determined to get him to loosen up.

"Spence, you got next," she told him.

"I'll be waiting at the bar."

Now once again, Jay and I were alone. I decided to take Lyric's advice and leave it alone about Autumn. I just wanted to enjoy myself without any drama. Jay was standing beside me as I sat in the chair.

"So you wanna dance?"

My body leaned back in the chair as I stared at him.

"Jay, you know I don't dance."

"You don't?"

"No, baby."

"So you saying you don't dance, or you can't dance?"

"Don't dance... usually."

"Come on and dance with me. Please?" Jay put his hand out for me to take. How could I resist? I got up and went with him out on the floor. I was glad they were at least playing a fast song. We didn't have to dance close, but then the music changed to something slow. Jay pulled me close, resting his hands near my ass, and we slow danced.

I just laughed at him as he played around with me while we were close. I was hoping he didn't feel a change in my weight, because I did have a little ball, but I loved being held by him and wasn't going to fight it. As my face eased into the curvature of his neck, I closed my eyes and tried to memorize everything about this moment.

I missed the closeness of the two of us. Most of all, I missed his touch. It had been so long since he'd made love to me, and I wanted that so bad, but knew I couldn't. I had to stick with my plan.

So for now, I'd drink in this moment, his scent, the way he felt, his hands touching my body non-intrusively, in hopes that he would remember me and that it happened very soon. I had to use the bathroom again. I sooo didn't want to break up this moment, but I had to pee.

"You just wanna leave?"

That request was music to my ears.

"I like that idea even better."

Once I came back from the bathroom, we let everyone know we were about to go. The girls, of course, were all smiles to see us leaving together. Unexpectedly, I felt nervous once I got to Jay's suite. I didn't know what to expect. Jay took his jacket off and his tee. He had a beater on underneath and was walking around in that.

I tried not to stare, but I couldn't help myself. I was like a moth to a flame when it came to his body, so it was hard trying to resist. His arms were so sculpted and inviting. I just loved his build, and it had been so long since I felt his touch, which made me afraid of being alone with him.

It was a balmy night from all the rain, so I could understand his discomfort. I, on the other hand, was already dressed for it. He opened the curtains and the sliding door on the terrace to let in the nighttime ambiance. Then he called and placed an order for room service.

"You want anything?"

"Sure!" He made it for two, and I told him what I wanted while he was on the line. Then I took my shoes off and got comfortable on the couch.

"What hotel you staying in?"

"Right here."

"Hold on one second." Jay's phone suddenly alerted him to

a text. I noticed two things. One, he didn't read it, and two, he turned the phone off. I got even more nervous about him fully giving me his attention. I hadn't had it in a while. When he set his phones down, I got up and walked out on the terrace since it was a beautiful night, considering the heat. Jay walked up and stood right behind me. He softly spoke in my ear as his lips lightly brushed it.

"Did I tell you how beautiful you look tonight?" My lips curved into a grin before I bit the corner of my bottom lip. His words alone gave me chills. I thought that was impossible seeing as though a wave of heat had me burning up on the inside.

"Not so much with words, but your eyes have said a lot," I managed to say. The tips of his fingers lightly sashayed down my arms while his lips hovered near my cheek.

"Yeah, they were checking you out. I haven't seen you dressed like this before."

God! I wanted to explode on the inside from the sinful way he was making me feel. I barely could smile from trying to hold it together as I spoke to him.

"I uh... I guess it has been awhile. I've been hospital gowning it lately."

Jay laughed. My hands were resting on the edge of the rail since I needed something to tightly squeeze. He gently put both his hands on top of mine as he stood pressed against my backside with his face now touching my cheek. The lump in my throat, I'm sure, became more apparent as I swallowed frequently, trying to suppress my nerves, as we gazed at the view of the city. We were on the fifty-second floor. I was in awe of the sparkling lights that showed a flash of color, which filled the skyline.

"Wow! Everything looks so tiny from up here, yet amazing."

"Baby."

"Yes."

"Would it be rude if I said I wanna fuck you right now?" I closed my eyes and took a deep breath. I wanted him so bad and missed when he would talk to me like this, but I didn't know how to respond. I was about to turn to face him, but Jay must've thought I was about to walk away and immediately grabbed my wrist, stopping me mid-turn. "Wait a minute!"

"No, I..."

"Don't leave!" I was about to explain to him that I was only turning to face him, but I didn't get a chance to. He had that look in his eyes again. They were so focused, like something else was occupying his mind.

"Jay, what are you thinking, baby?"

"We were out on a balcony before. Were we on a boat?"

"Yes, Jay, we were. Several times actually."

"You were crying and about to walk away from me, but I stopped you." His eyes were so intense as he stared at me while his mind was pondering on events. "Shanell, were we ever really happy?"

My body relaxed on the rail once Jay let me go.

"Yes, Jay, we were. I know it probably seems like you're remembering a lot of the bad times, but baby, we were happy.

I lost a lot of my confidence and had low self-esteem when El did that to me. Nikki was really coming on strong with you during that time frame, and I just wanted to give up and let her win. I didn't know why you wanted me in your life anymore, but you wouldn't let me leave. You made me stay there and talk to you. Baby, we may have had our ups and downs. but Jay, we always found a way to get through it."

His eyes searched my face.

"I just feel like I'm always hurting you."

"Jay, that's not true." At this point, I grabbed his hands and leaned into him. "Jay, I've never been happier than I've been since the day I met you. Baby, I was going to be your wife. I wasn't going anywhere, and I'm still not, Jay, unless you want me to."

"Man, these memories of us are very powerful. It's like when I'm in that moment, I can feel every emotion that took place. Like ya pain when you were crying. I felt that shit. Then the moment disappeared, and I'm back to now, left with the memory of it but kinda detached from the feeling. I know that might sound crazy, but I swear it's the weirdest thing."

"No, it doesn't sound crazy at all."

"So we gon' work on this or what?"

I had to make sure I was hearing correctly.

"What'd you say?"

"I wanna give us a chance, Shanell."

"Jay, do you mean it?"

"I think I do. I know I don't have all my memory back yet, but when I saw you here tonight, everything felt right.

I'm not saying I want us to rush back into things as far as the wedding and shit, but I do wanna explore what we had."

My emotions got the best of me as they tended to do most of the time, and my eyes began to water. I was so overjoyed that he wanted to take things slow in hopes to get back what we shared before. This was something that I didn't anticipate happening, which meant I had to decide if I was going to just tell him about the pregnancy, without him having all his memory.

"Jay I'm—"

He suddenly kissed me. It was with so much passion my body was on overload and about to malfunction. He woke up so many things in me that had been suppressed for a minute. Suddenly, our connection was interrupted by a knock on the door. The food had finally arrived. I quickly dried my eyes and gathered myself while Jay went to go answer the door.

Jay

"Yo, man, what took y'all so long?"

"I do apologize, sir. We are running behind with some of the orders, but you'll notice a discounted rate on your bill."

"Now we talking. Good looking out." We had a seat at the table and ate. "Are you staying until tomorrow too?"

"I am."

"When ya flight scheduled to leave?"

"Not until 2:00 pm."

"Mine ain't until that night at 9:45 pm. Maybe I could see if I could get it changed so we could fly back together."

She smiled so big.

"Maybe you should."

She told me more about our relationship while we ate. How we met and more about our time spent together on both cruises. I felt like I never knew anyone like her. I was proud to know her. Since I was already half dressed and sweaty as shit from all the heat surrounding me, I wanted to take a shower.

"You mind if I hopped in the shower real quick?"

"Not at all."

"You can join me if you like."

Her eyes lit up and her lips curled into a smile.

"That's all you. I'm good."

"You sure? I know I'm not the only one feeling hot and shit."

She shook her head as she answered.

"No, I'm definitely hot, but this water will suffice. You go ahead."

I grabbed a few things out of my room first and then got in the shower. While I was in there, Shanell came in and told me she needed to run to her room for a second and would be back.

"Wait! I'm 'bouta get out. Lemme come with you."

"Jay, I'll be fine."

She left just like that. I got out, and she was gone. I decided to check my phones real quick since I turned them off. I noticed text messages from Autumn and Nikki. Autumn's read: *Noticed you had left early. Never got a chance to say* *goodnight. Don't wanna sleep without hearing ya voice luv. Call me <3*

"This girl crazy." Then I read Nikki's. *Thinking of you as I sit here reading to our little one. We love you & can't wait to see you when you come back. Looking forward to our talk. Kiss! Kiss!* "Yeah, we definitely gonna talk."

I was still only in a towel when Shanell knocked on the door. When I opened it, I noticed the smirk on her face as she was enjoying the view. I also noticed she had her things in her hand.

"You didn't needa get that. What you need night clothes on for?"

She smiled and patted my chest.

"We're taking it slow, remember?"

"It don't gotta be that slow."

"Yes, it does," she emphatically assured.

I looked down at the imprint my shit made in the towel.

"Damn! No love for you tonight." Shanell burst into laughter. It was so infectious I laughed too.

Chapter Ten

TEMPERATURE RISING

Shanell

The woman in me wanted him to make love to me so bad, but I was afraid for him to see my body exposed since he didn't know I was pregnant. I was really regretting hiding it in the first place now. Hopefully, with bits and pieces of things jogging his memory, it would be a matter of time before he remembered how much I meant to him, so I could tell him. Jay went and put his boxers on while I went in the bathroom to get comfortable. It was real late, and I was tiring out.

"Babe, I'm going to bed."

"I'm right behind you."

We got in the bed and spooned for a bit. His arms cuddling me felt perfect. If I didn't sleep at all tonight, it would be worth it because I wanted to live in this feeling always.

The next morning when I awoke, Jay was sitting at the table in the room writing. I sat up in the bed and noticed next to him was a basket of fresh fruit and a hot plate. Jay looked in my direction. He saw I had awakened and showed me his beautiful smile.

"Aye!" He got up and came over to me. "Good morning," he said then kissed my cheek.

"Good morning."

"I got some breakfast over there if you're hungry."

Jay walked back to the table while I got out the bed and went in the bathroom to freshen up. Once I was done, I joined him. He took the lid off the plate to show me what I had, which was toast, eggs, sausage and some potatoes. It also was a small container of yogurt on the side. I loved the gesture, but my stomach was still trying to recuperate from what we had eaten late last night. I didn't want to seem unappreciative, so I decided to eat on the yogurt.

"What's wrong? You're not hungry?"

"I'm still kinda full from last night. This is fine though. What were you doing?"

"I'm just writing down some things I wanna run by Kyle."

This fine specimen of a man... I just couldn't take my eyes

off and stared at Jay lovingly for a few seconds as he wrote. Then I went back to eating my yogurt.

"How'd it feel being back in the studio? Did you sing anything just for practice?"

"Yeah, he actually had me going over 'Loving You'. I also listened to a lot of other songs that I recorded. It was nice. Kyle is good, man. I was impressed with everything he showed me."

"Yeah, Kyle has taught you a lot, Jay." I looked at my watch and noticed the time. I jumped up from the table. "Oh my gosh! Jay, I gotta go. I have to get my things together and get dressed."

Jay walked over to me, remaining calm.

"Baby, hold on. You gon' have time to do that."

"I didn't realize it was this late. You know my flight leaves at 2:00 pm."

"Won't you see if you can change it so you can leave with me tonight?"

"I thought you were going to see about changing yours so you could fly home with me?"

"I did, but ya flight is booked."

"Aw, babe."

Jay moved in a little closer to me. The tone in his voice turned sensual.

"Come on... stay with me."

"You're horny, aren't you?" He pushed his body even closer, and I felt his firmness. "Jay please don't do this to me," I said, flustered.

"It ain't me," he defended playfully. "He has a mind of his own." Jay tried to lift my top. I almost had a heart attack.

"Jay, no!" I tried to ease away from him, but his hands were all over me. "No seriously," I squealed. "We're taking things slow, remember?"

"Alright, I understand."

He left me alone so I could gather my things. He was checking his phones in the meantime.

"Okay. I think I have everything."

I walked over and kissed Jay real quick on the lips.

"Hold on. I'mma walk with you." Jay threw on some clothes and walked me to my floor. We stood outside of my room for a minute.

"So I guess I won't be seeing you until you get home tonight."

"Yeah, you'll probably be sleep doe."

"Yeah, if I'm tired. It won't be that late when you arrive."

"Right! The time differences. I keep forgettin'. So does this mean I can come back in the room to sleep?"

"Mm, maybe."

"Shid, I'm sleeping wit' dat ass."

"Come here." I guided his chin to my lips and kissed him. "I'll see you at home." As much as I didn't want us to separate, I opened the door and went inside. When I walked in, Nevaeh was coming out of the bathroom.

"Somebody looks like they had a good ass night."

I sat in the chair, distraught.

"I'm in deep shit!"

She stood in front of me.

"Oh, Lord, cousin, what now?"

"Jay wants to work things out."

She narrowed her eyes in confusion.

"So where's the problem?"

"I'm scared to tell him that I'm pregnant. I came so close to it last night," I whined.

"So what stopped you?"

My eyes looked up at her.

"His lips. Ugh!" I pouted as I threw myself back against the seat. "I don't know what to do. I didn't plan on this happening without him remembering us completely."

"Shanell, what difference does it make? He probably would be happy to know that he's going to be a father to a child with you."

"What if he's not, because of Nikki being pregnant? At least if he had his memory, Nevaeh, he would know what he's really dealing with when it comes to me. He would know that he wanted to spend the rest of his life with me and would probably feel better about hearing that I'm pregnant too, since he possibly has one on the way. Now if I tell him, I don't know how he's gonna feel about it. Plus, it's twins at that."

"Look, just tell him. You have to deal with this one way or another. It's time, Shanell. You need to tell him."

Autumn

"Hello."

"Bitch, what the fuck are you doing?" I yelled.

"What? What are you talking about?"

"Are you sleeping underneath a rock? They're getting close again."

"No, they're not. He barely remembers her."

"Do I have to do everything including think for your ass? She came to *Fallchester City,* and they were together... looking very happy I might add. You're not holding up to your end of the deal."

"Yes, I am. How do you know she's in *Fallchester City* with him?"

"See, that's what I'm talking about. You should've known that information. Let's not forget you wanted in on this, but if you can't hold up to your end, then tell me now!"

"Bitch, don't try to act all high and mighty! You can't even get close to Jay without the things that I do. You've known her every move thus far, so don't get it twisted on who needs who."

"I just want to be with him. She doesn't make him happy."

"And you think I want her around? I can't stand her entitled ass as much as you don't want them together! Yet I play the role."

"Well, I thought you should know she was here and seeing as though she is, I'm going to set a few more things in place of my own to move this along."

"Do that! The clock is ticking on my patience."

"Believe me. Mine too."

"Find out when she'll be returning and if Jay will be accompanying her. Let me know as soon as you find out.

"I'll be in touch."

Jay

Before I left *Fallchester*, I wanted to have a talk with Autumn since I was going to wholeheartedly work on things with Shanell. I didn't want to leave any loose ends, so I planned on making the stop to her hotel a quick one, since I still needed to finish packing. I called her first to see what she was up to. We spoke for a few, before I was on my way. When I arrived, it took her a few minutes to answer. I was 'bouta leave when she finally opened the door.

"Sorry it took me so long. I was in the bathroom." I noticed she was wrapped in a towel. Not the sight I was expecting to see at all. Autumn's hair had beads of water dripping from it as it fell on her wet neck, making her skin glow. I could smell the scent of sweet strawberries that lingered from it. My eyes were glued to her as the towel hugged every curve of her body and exposed her damp, caramel colored skin.

"Fuck!"

"Do come in."

I couldn't take my eyes off her as she dripped with sex appeal.

"Maybe I shouldn't. You should probably get some clothes on first."

Autumn grabbed my hand and pulled me inside. Her face had this cunning look and seemingly one thing on her mind. She dropped her towel to the floor once the door was shut. I was still standing in front of it, not sure if I should continue to stare or tear myself away from her.

"Uh... Autumn, I just..."

She pressed her naked body and then her lips against me, making me fall back against the door. I was so caught off guard I never had a chance. We continued to kiss, and then Autumn started lifting my shirt up suggesting me to take it off. I did. She then began to walk backwards to the bed, signaling me with her pointer finger to come to her. I was so fuckin' horny, I followed.

Her naked body was laid out on the bed, eagerly waiting for me to get on top of it. I quickly unfastened my pants and took everything off. Lastly, I pulled a condom from my wallet and prepared to put it on, but Autumn wanted the honors. She took it from my hand and ripped it open with her mouth. As I stood in front of her, she made sure to take her time as she enjoyed feeling my swelled, hard tool in her hand. Then she slid back in position in the middle of the bed and took her fingers and plunged into herself, giving me a pre-show. That shit had me so fuckin' turned on I was ready to be a part of it.

With no words spoken but body language very clear, I moved my body to Autumn's and filled the gap in between her legs. She rested them on my shoulders as her pussy stared me in the face while she continued to pleasure herself. There was only one thing left that I needed to do... which was take over the show and pleasure her myself.

Shanell

We finally arrived at *Velport Airport*. Evan was going to go and get the car and bring it up, but we all outnumbered him in choosing to wait for the shuttle and ride it to the parking lot. There was a small section of street in front of the airport separated by the median where you stood to catch certain shuttles.

As the four of us were crossing, a black car with tinted windows came speeding out of nowhere looking to hit us. Evan and Marcus hurriedly pushed Nevaeh and me out of the way, making us both fall to the ground as they quickly got out of harm's way. The car swerved, missing Evan and Marcus by inches and kept on going.

I was slow to get up. Nevaeh noticed me still on the ground just sitting there rocking back and forth in tears. She finally was able to get herself up from the small grassy patch that she landed on and ran over to me.

"Shanell! Oh my God! What's wrong?" She noticed I was hugging my elbows with my hands. My elbows and arms were all scraped up from the way I landed. "Oh my gosh, cousin!"

Marcus and Evan ran over to me to see what was wrong. They both noticed my arms bloody and skin scraped away. I landed on them so I wouldn't fall on my stomach and in doing so slid on the cement which peeled my skin away. They were furious.

"Dammit! Damnit! Damnit!" yelled Evan.

Marcus came to my side.

"Fuckin' shit, man! Did you get hurt anywhere else?" I couldn't even talk from crying because it was burning so bad, so I shook my head no. Then Marcus looked at Nevaeh. "Are you okay? You in pain anywhere?"

"No, but she needs to get to the hospital Marcus, right away."

"Yeah, you both should be checked out as a precaution."

"Marcus, I'm fine."

"Didn't you just have surgery on ya back not too long ago?"

"Yeah, but really I'm okay. Shanell's the one that really needs it."

"Can you please just get checked out for me? I just need to know for sure that you both are okay."

Nevaeh didn't refuse him anymore. She agreed to be seen too.

Evan

"Shanell, do not move until an ambulance comes," Evan ordered.

I then walked back across the street. I couldn't stop

thinking about the vehicle that tried to run all us over. I was pissed that I couldn't get a license plate number since there was none on the back of the car. They had it in the windshield, but the windows were so tinted you couldn't make out the numbers.

I decided to see if anyone else noticed anything at all that may have stood out with the car. Shortly after, airport security came to ask some questions. They had already called for an ambulance since they were notified about a few victims possibly being hurt. The ambulance was there in no time. I stayed and spoke with security while Marcus went ahead with Nevaeh and Shanell to the hospital.

Shanell

Once we arrived and I was seen they noticed immediately that my blood pressure was up. Then they gave me an ultrasound to check on the babies, which seemed to be okay. Next, I was treated for my injuries to my arms. As a precaution, they decided to admit me and monitor me overnight just to keep an eye on my blood pressure and to make sure everything else was okay since I previously was in a coma. The doctor told me if all signs were a go, I would be able to leave the next day.

Nevaeh was examined and was found to be okay. She did get prescribed some pain medicine. Then we got separated when I got put in a room. Marcus was already in here after he was allowed to come in.

Marcus

"Hey! What did the doc—"

I saw a monitor hooked up to her stomach and was speechless. She was sitting in the bed crying. I thought maybe she just found out that she was pregnant and was upset about it. I really didn't know what to say. I was so happy when Nevaeh came in the room.

She rolled her neck at me concerned, like I did something.

"What's wrong with her?"

I pulled Nevaeh over by the door.

"Yo, I think she upset because she found out she pregnant."

"What?"

"No fo'real. I'm just as surprised as you. If you look, there's a monitor on her stomach, and that can only be there for one reason. I'mma leave you in here so y'all can talk. I don't know what to say to her at this point."

"Okay, let me talk to her."

Shanell

When Marcus walked out the door, Nevaeh came over to me. I was just lying there looking spaced out I'm sure, drying my tears every so often. Nevaeh sat in the chair.

"Did you hear any of that?"

"Yeah, I heard him," I answered, not staring at her.

"So now that he knows too, what are you going to do?"

"I can't even think about that right now." I finally looked at her. "What the hell just happened to us out there? Do you know?"

"No. Evan is looking into it, and then he'll be here to get us. I'd like to know that my damn self."

"I could've lost my babies, Nevaeh. Who would do something like that?"

"I don't know. They just came plowing out of nowhere while all of us were crossing."

"Nevaeh, I'm starting to think none of these things are accidents. I believe someone is trying to hurt me."

"But why you? We all were crossing the street."

"This isn't the first time something crazy like this has happened. Did I tell you not too long ago somebody also left some dead black roses on my car, and they busted the windshield too."

"No, cousin."

"Yes. Marcus gave me some bogus story about it being an accident. He said some girl meant to do that to someone else's car that looked like mine. I didn't believe it completely at the time, but I just let it go. Now this happens."

"That does seem strange. What did Jay say?"

"He was the main one telling me not to worry about it. That if stuff like that keeps happening, then be concerned. After this... I'm concerned."

Nevaeh looked like a few things were going through her mind.

"Looks like we need to see about getting some answers from Marcus."

"It seems like all of these things started happening the

minute me and Jay got engaged. Nevaeh, what if it's El? What if he's escaped and wants to kill me for setting him up?"

"Shanell, please don't get all worked up. El's ass is locked up. He's not that clever to escape."

"But what if he's not locked up? He found a way to get out before. Maybe they found some evidence that could get him out early... maybe—"

"Cousin, please try to relax. Your blood pressure is rising, and you're going to work yourself into a panic attack."

I raised my tone an octave.

"How can I relax when someone is trying to hurt me?" Then I got to thinking about the coma. "Nevaeh, how did I get in that coma? No one never wanted to tell me."

"God, I was hoping you wouldn't ask me about that because it just dawned on me that you could be on to something... unfortunately, you could be right. It seems they found morphine in your system, but before you panic," she said lifting her hands. "They're investigating it because they were thinking it was malpractice."

"Oh my God!" I panicked. "Someone is trying to kill me! That's probably why that cop was outside of my door." My eyes welled up with more tears. I was filled with fear once again. "I really need Jay. I need him here so bad."

Nevaeh got up and comforted me. Marcus made it back in the room and was accompanied by Evan. They both walked over and stood by the end of the bed. I dried my eyes and gathered myself. Then I seriously looked at Evan and Marcus.

"You two know more about what's going on than what you have been telling me. Right now! I need the truth."

"Look, Shanell, we're trying to get to the bottom of this," Evan explained. "We don't know who that was in the car and why that happened."

"But you do know that someone is trying to hurt me, don't you?" Evan and Marcus looked at one another.

Marcus

I know we were told by Jay not to say anything, but I wasn't so sure anymore, especially now in her condition. I felt she should know for her own safety. Evan, on the other hand, I knew wasn't aware of the new developments yet, so I knew it wouldn't be easy for him to give up any information to Shanell and go against Jay's orders.

"Shanell, someone has been posing as a threat to you. We don't know why or who it is, but we're doing our damnedest to keep you safe."

Evan's eyes were cutting into me so hard. I bet he was wondering why I said something.

"So, Jay knows about this already?"

Evan continued to look at me. He frowned at me and nodded, swaying his hand for me to continue what I started.

"Shanell, he only was protecting you. He didn't want you to be afraid and worrying about doing your day to day routines all the time."

That got Nevaeh worked up.

"Who does Jay think he is? This is very serious! She should've been informed if for nothing else, so she could be aware of any danger that could arise and not be blindsided like now."

Evan was quick to say something in Jay's defense.

"Shanell, we were only doing our job, and we're going to continue to do that. Me and Marcus will lay down our lives first before we allow anything to happen to you. Jay really only did what he thought was best."

Shanell

I didn't have anything else to say. I couldn't believe that Jay knew and kept it from me when we discussed how I despised him doing this same thing with the El situation. And he couldn't use his memory loss as an excuse, because he knew this beforehand.

"Nevaeh and Evan, do you mind if I speak to Marcus alone?" They both walked out of the room so I could talk with Marcus. He sat beside me on the bed. "Does Evan know now that I'm pregnant too?"

"He does if he noticed that monitor hooked up to you like that. Other than that, I

don't know."

"Well if he doesn't, I don't want you to say anything. I also don't want you to say anything to Jay."

"I mean, it's not my place to say anything anyway, but why would you not want to tell Jay?"

"Look, Marcus, you kept his secret. Do me a favor and keep mine."

"Let me say something to you as a man. I would never be able to forgive a woman who knowingly kept a child from me when she knew I wanted to be a father."

"I'm not keeping it from him, Marcus. It's just for now."

"I swear I never saw two people love each other as much as you two do, but constantly keep information from each other, thinking it's for their own good. You're sure you're not thinking about getting an abortion or anything?"

"No! Why would you think that?"

"Aw, man!" he said looking relieved. "Because you were crying and shit like it was bad news. I didn't know what to say to you."

"No, I'm not getting an abortion. You wanna know something? I found out we're actually having twins."

"Damn! Double duty." I laughed. "Well, sweetheart, congratulations. I promise you, Shanell, I will not let anything happen to you or them babies." Marcus sat there with a big smile on his face. "You gotta hurry up and tell my man though. I gotta get him some cigars for when I congratulate him."

"I'm going to tell him. I just need to do it in my own time."

"Can I say something else?"

"What?"

"I noticed you picked up a little weight. I didn't wanna say anything because I don't say stuff like that to women. Plus, I thought it might've had to do with you being in the hospital so long, but as far as time goes... you don't have much. That's gonna be a dead giveaway pretty soon."

"Yeah, I know."

"But as far as this other situation goes, we on top of it. The police are aware of what's been going on, so just know we're gonna get whoever is behind this. I promise you."

"Oh, I can't wait for Jaylen to get here." I growled.

"Ut oh! That mean somebody in the doghouse."

"Oh, Marcus, you can't even imagine how I'm feeling right now... can't *even* imagine."

Chapter Eleven

YOUR BABY

*L**yric*

Me and Sienna were waiting in Jay's suite for him to come back.

"Sienna, where did Jay go?"

"Him and Spence had to go somewhere real quick before we left."

"He knows he needs to finish packing. He betta get here soon."

"I know, but that's Jay sometimes. Always needing to do something at thc last minute."

Jay

I still hadn't left Autumn's room yet. I was just about to

pull up my boxers when my cell phone went off. I noticed it was E and answered it. He explained to me what happened, and I stood in disbelief.

"What she doing now?"

"She in the room talking to Marcus."

"E, man, let her know I'll be there as soon as I can.

Suddenly guilt started to seep in. I picked up the rest of my clothes off the floor and sat on the edge of the bed and put them on. Autumn sat up and crawled behind me trying to still kiss on my neck as I got dressed. I shook her off me. She just paused as she stared at me.

"Why you lookin' at me like that?" I asked.

"I can't get another hit before you dip on me?"

I sighed.

"I gotta go, man."

Fucking her again was the last thing on my mind.

"I'll see you back in *Velport* then. Maybe we could pick it up there."

I had just put my sneaker on when she said that.

"Yeah, about that. I'mma be wit' my baby, so you gon' hafta chill with the text messages and phone calls." I was standing up by now and about to head to the door. Autumn looked dumbfounded like her feelings were hurt.

"Your baby?"

I turned around.

"I ain't stutter."

Autumn hurried up and got off the bed and picked up her robe to put it on.

"Oh, really, Jay? It's like that now?"

"Come on now, Autumn. I'm not serious about you. You know that."

"Oh, so I'm just an ear when you need it and a piece of ass for you to fuck?"

"You knew what it was before I got here, man." I opened the door. "Later." I left. She slammed the door behind me.

Autumn

"Ooo!" I was pissed! I rested my head in the palm of my hand for a second. I couldn't believe he played me like this! I opened the door back up to go after him, but once I looked both ways, I saw he had gone. "Ahhhh!" I screamed, slamming the door back closed again. I didn't let my anger or disappointment consume me for long. I grabbed my phone.

"Hey! Jay just left, and I think it was due to a phone call he got. Were you able to intercept her at the airport?"

"Yeah, but her bodyguards were too close for me to hit her ass, but she damn sure hit the ground hard."

"Good! I have something too that's sure to ruin their relationship. I'll give you details later."

"Okay!"

I walked over to the small digital camera I had set up in the room and stopped it. I knew I had our little encounter recorded. He never even noticed it, just like I expected.

"Looks like I'm not the only one that just got fucked!"

Shanell

Marcus got in touch with Jay to let him know that I said not to worry about coming to the hospital until the morning. I would be going home, so once Jay got in that Sunday night, he went home. I was hoping Marcus got the message to him in time and that he would actually listen and not show up, or else my secret would've been exposed. Lucky for me he listened.

Nikki

I was at the hospital in the morning and stumbled across Shanell being admitted that previous day. Discreetly, I looked at her info and found out why she was brought in.

"Hm." I read what she was being treated for, but I wanted to know exactly what happened. That made me mosey over to see who worked in ER last night so I could get some info without causing suspicion. Luckily for me, people were already talking about it because they knew Shanell's association to Jay, and this was more gossip. When I found out all I needed to know, I immediately took my break and made a phone call.

Jay

In the morning, I rode over to the hospital to pick Shanell

up. I did as she asked since I was assured that she was okay. I walked in the room and saw her sitting on the edge of the bed, dressed and ready. Relief spilled all over my face. I knew already that she was okay, but to see her now in my presence calmed and soothed my spirit.

Relief was accompanied with a smile as I walked over to her, kissed her cheek and sat beside her. Truth be told, I was glad that I didn't have to come by here last night. I wasn't ready to face her after I'd just had sex with Autumn and here, she was going through this shit. I had to put that out my mind like it never happened.

"You ain't joking 'bout always being up in here are you?"

She rolled her eyes at me, not amused.

"Well believe me, it's definitely not by choice."

"Lemme see ya arms?"

She pulled a little of the bandage back so I could see what happened."

"Damn, girl. I bet that shit did hurt."

"Who you telling?"

"They kept you here overnight for that though?"

"Well, my blood pressure was up too, and considering the coma, they just were being cautious."

"That's understandable. So you didn't injure yourself anywhere else?"

"No."

"Man, I can't even believe somebody did that shit to y'all."

Shanell hopped up off the bed.

"Yeah, well me either, but we'll finish this conversation at home. I'm ready to get out of here."

She led the way, and I followed behind her to leave. She was quiet the whole drive. I knew something was bothering her, and my guess it was about what happened. Once we got in, Shanell decided to go take a nice hot bubble bath. I told her I was going to be in the office. Shortly after, Momma had come down the stairs and noticed I was back. She walked in the office.

"Hey, baby."

"Hey Momma."

"Where's Shanell?"

"She upstairs in the tub."

"How is she?"

"She gon' be alright. She messed up her arms real bad doe."

"That girl always seems to have something happening to her. It's so sad."

"It seems like she handles it pretty well though."

"Jay, is it possible that the same person that put her in that coma is the same person that tried to hit her?"

"I hate to admit it, but I know it's the same person. Nothing else makes sense. I just wish I knew who that was and why they're doing this."

"Baby, if Shanell doesn't already know that she's in danger, you need to tell her."

"I thought keeping it from her was a good idea since she was in the hospital, but I guess now I have to tell her."

"Yeah, Jay, I think that's a good idea. Have you been having anymore flashbacks?"

"It's funny you mention that because I had some things come to me again in *Fallchester*."

"What was it this time?"

"Same type of memories. Always dealing with me and Shanell."

"I'm just glad to hear your mind is triggering something from before. I'm sure this is frustrating for you as you go through this, but hopefully it won't be too much longer."

"I know... Momma, Kyle told me something about live videos I used to do to connect with my fans. You know anything about that?"

"Yeah, baby. You think you wanna go live?"

"Yeah. What you think?"

"Jay, I think it's a good idea and really overdue. You don't know this, but you've received tons of gifts and well wishes since the accident from your fans. Now since the cops are monitoring the fan club right now and its activity, you won't get to see any of it. But I think it's time you let them know that you're okay and to thank them."

"You know, it really bothers me to know that one of my fans or it may even be a few of them out to hurt Shanell."

"I know, baby. Unfortunately, it's some sick people out there who can't differentiate your brand from the man behind the brand. They feel like you're not entitled to have a personal life."

"But I'm human too, Momma. I'm supposed to be

excluded from being happy just to continue to make them happy?"

"I know... believe me. I know where you're coming from."

"I wouldn't wish a life like that for nobody."

"No. Neither would I. A lot of people don't feel that way though, but there are quite a few that do. Unfortunately, Jay, there's nothing you can do about it."

I just sat there for a minute feeling discouraged.

"So what I needa do to get on here?"

"Well, first we'll make an announcement on your social media pages. Here, let me show you." Momma leaned over and showed me what to do on my phone. I thought I could get on now, but she told me to give my fans some time to see the message so they could join me. I decided to do it in a few hours then, so I set it up for later.

Shanell was finally out of the tub and dressed. She came downstairs and saw Momma in the office with me. They started talking, and eventually she showed her what happened to her arms.

"Sweetheart, I'm so glad you're going to be okay." She gave her a hug. "Well, I have some errands to run, so I'll see the both of you later. Jay, if you have any problems going live, if I'm not back, call me, or ask Shanell.

"You're going live today?"

"Yeah. I thought I'd say a lil' something to my fans and let 'em know a few updates."

"Jay, can we talk?"

"Yeah... come sit down." I got up, and we both went to sit

on the sofa. Shanell sat with her hands in her lap. I could tell this talk was going to be serious.

"Jay, it's really kinda difficult to have this conversation with you when you don't have your memory back to know what I have a problem with." She took a deep breath. "Okay, what I'm trying to say is—"

"You know, don't you?"

"About someone trying to threaten my life... yes!"

"Shanell, I was going to talk to you about it aft—" I paused. "After..." All of a sudden, my brain went on an information overload, putting me in a trance. I felt like I was right back in the place I was before when I was telling Shanell about me sleeping with Nikki and her possibly being pregnant. It was déjà vu, but this time I remembered everything. Shanell was asking me if something else had come to me, but my brain was still processing memories. I couldn't speak.

"Jay... baby, talk to me. Did you just remember something?" I was looking at Shanell as if it was my first time seeing her in a long time. All I could do was smile. I was back. I wanted to grab her up and let her know I got my memory back, but I wasn't completely sure if I wanted to tell her now like this. I decided to wait and share it with Momma first. Then it hit me when I noticed she was no longer wearing her engagement ring. I remembered I called it off. I knew I had to get that put back where it belonged. Shanell broke my thoughts when she called me again.

"Jaylen!"

"I'm sorry... What I do?" I asked, still smiling as I saw my world right in front of me.

"You just scared me! You were talking and then just stopped like something was wrong."

"What was I was saying?"

"Stop smiling at me like that! You know I'm upset with you right now, and memory or not, I'm not letting this slide." I couldn't help himself and went in for a kiss. I was filled with so many emotions and lots of love in my heart for this woman that sat beside me that I couldn't contain myself. She let me kiss her, but she still wasn't letting what I did go.

"I'm sorry. I just had to do that."

"Jay, this is serious. Me and you discussed you not keeping information from me, and you turned around and did it again." I had to really think about what we were just talking about before my brain went on sudden overload. Then it came to me about saying that I was going to tell her that she was right about someone trying to cause her harm, and I did, again, keep it from her. But I was so happy I couldn't focus on having that conversation at the moment. I knew it was a serious matter, but I just wanted to keep my spirits high and relish having the missing pieces that were finally given back to me.

"Baby, listen to me. I know you wanna talk about this and how I fucked up again, and I don't blame you for being upset. But can we discuss this later tonight? I promise you we'll talk about it."

"Jay, what's wrong with now?"

"I don't want you to be mad at me right now."

"Oh, so I can be mad at you later?"

"You ain't gon' be able to be mad at me later." Shanell laughed.

"You think you slick. And why won't I be mad later, Jay? I didn't say you were coming back in the bedroom yet."

"Shid! You definitely ain't keeping me away from you tonight."

Shanell

That scared me a bit. He was too confident about that, unlike before. That response seemed more like my baby talking. I loved when that side of him would show, but with my body going through these changes, I knew I had to be careful in the bed with Jay. But I figured it'd be fine. We were only going to cuddle like before. Jay started nuzzling his face in my neck. Then his lips gave me small pecks. He had me so turned on.

"Damn, girl, you gettin' my fuckin' dick hard."

I was taken aback. He really was starting to sound like himself again. From the sounds of things, he wasn't trying to take it slow at all, and honestly, I didn't want to either. I just had to find the courage to tell him I'm pregnant.

"Well, I'm... I'm known to have that uh, effect on you."

I had to get away from him, so I eased out the seat just to create some distance.

"So you gon' leave me feeling like this?"

"What's gotten into you?"

Jay got right back in my space again.

"Why you keep moving away from me? What, I needa brush my teeth again or something?" I cracked up.

"No!"

"So, what's the problem? You all jumpy and shit." I moved away again since Jay wouldn't keep his hands off me.

"No, I'm not." Jay came close to me again. This time from behind, grabbing me at the hips. With his lips close to my face, he spoke softly in my ear, letting his lips slightly brush my skin, knowing what that did to me.

"Come get in the pool with me?"

"Jay, I just got out the tub."

He turned me around and slowly rolled his tongue over his bottom lip as those hazel eyes tried to do a number on me as I stared in them.

"You can't get wet for me again?"

I was kicking myself on the inside. He had me incredibly aroused. Wet was beyond what I was for him, but I knew I had to focus and bring it back.

"I gotta go over to the condo, babe. Nevaeh is waiting for me." He sighed, not liking that.

"Alright." He let me go. "We'll pick this back up tonight." I looked at him, boggled, and then went and got my purse to go over to the condo. I made up my mind that tonight when we talked, I was going to tell him everything.

Jay

It was time for me to go live and talk to my fans. Momma wasn't back yet from being out, but Sienna was now with me. I pretty much knew what to do because I had my memory back, but no one knew it yet. I didn't see a problem with Sienna assisting me, so I went with the flow, but I was always grateful for her and all the things she did for me.

Before I went live, she told me what would happen and what'd I see once I appeared and also what to do to respond. The minute I got on, they were going crazy with comments. It made me smile.

"I know a nigga been out of commission for a bit, but I'm back. Just wanna get on here and thank y'all for the get-well cards and the gifts and shit that were sent. Y'all don't know how much that meant to me, man. 'Preciate dat shit. But I'm doing great... feeling pretty good... 'bout to get back on my grind again... so um, I wanted to fill y'all in on what a nigga been doing since my accident." I had to laugh at myself for a second. "I fucked my shit up... but it's all good doe..." Then I started responding to some of the comments. "Nah. but I'm just getting back in the swing of things. I did a video for 'Loving You', so y'all can expect to be seeing that pretty soon... what else... I actually been doing some more writing lately, so I'm saying this to y'all, and I haven't even spoke to Kyle yet, but I'm ready to work on my next album." Sienna nodded her head, impressed with the way I was handling things. If she only knew. "Sienna, can you bring me some water please?"

"Sure, Jay."

She left out the room.

"So I just wanted to get on here real quick to thank y'all and let y'all know that I love each and every one of you... Thanks again for all the love and support you show a nigga... Oh, before I go, because I see a lot of y'all asking about Shanell. Shanell is doing fine, and things with me and her are good. I'mma leave it at that. Muah! Alright, I'm out!"

By then, Sienna was back waiting for me to get done talking before she handed me my water.

"Jay, if I didn't know any better, I would think you got your memory back. But I'd like to think you wouldn't hide something as big as that."

I guzzled that shit down for a second before I responded to her.

"Sienna, I wasn't hiding it. I didn't wanna say anything until I talked to Momma first."

"Jay, so you *do* have your memory back?"

"Ya boy is back!"

I hugged her.

"Oh my gosh! It's about freakin' time! Wait! Let me make sure. Do you remember telling me I could get a raise?"

"I never said that shit."

"Yeah, you got your memory back. Oh, I bet Ms. Murphy is gonna be so happy! Oh my gosh," she said, smacking her cheeks. "Shanell is gonna trip!"

"Yeah, about that. I wanna do something special for her when I tell her, so I don't want you to say anything yet."

"Ugh!" She folded her arms and shook her head. "Okay. My lips are sealed. So, do you even know what you wanna do for her?"

"Nah, I still gotta think about it. I know I hurt her when I called the engagement off, so I really wanna make it up to her."

"Aw, Jay, that is so sweet."

Suddenly, Momma walked in and spoke to the two of us.

"So how'd going live go?" I couldn't stop smiling at this beautiful queen that I had so much love for. I walked over to her, picked her up, swung her around, and gave her a big kiss. "What was that for?"

"Momma, I'm back."

"You're back," she asked as her feet were placed back on the floor. Then it dawned on her what I was talking about. "Jay, you're back? You got your memory back?"

"I got it back. All of it."

Momma grabbed me up so tight she had tears in her eyes because she was so happy.

"Aw, Momma, don't cry." I embraced her even more. Her crying had me all tearful and shit. She was at a loss for words for a minute, then she looked up at me as I held her.

"God, I'm so happy. I tried not to lose hope that you would get all your memory back, and now you finally have it. God is so good!"

"I love you, Momma."

"I love you too, baby." I hugged her once more. She kissed my cheek and dried her eyes. "So how'd it happen?" We walked over to the sofa so we could sit down and talk. I explained to her the conversation Shanell and I had and how in the middle of it, everything came back.

"So Shanell knows, and she's not here?"

"Not exactly. I haven't told her yet. I wanted to do something special for her to let her know."

"She is gonna be so happy."

"Yeah, so we gon' keep this from her for a little bit until I can figure out what I wanna do."

"You know this isn't going to be easy for me, right? I hope whatever you decide to do, you do it quick. Oh, I gotta go call your sister and your aunt."

"Let me do it."

My aunt got so emotional once I told her the news. That phone call made her day. Then she put Janae on. We talked for a good while. I missed that girl. Talking to her made me work up an appetite. I hung up and walked to the fridge to eat some leftovers.

While I was eating, the doorbell rang. Momma was upstairs and Sienna had left to pick up a few things I needed so I got up and walked to go answer it. It was Nikki. I couldn't believe she just showed up to my house like that. She had me heated like a muhfucker.

"What you doing here?"

"You wanted us to talk when you got back, remember? I just saw you on live and realized you were home, so I thought I'd come to you."

I forgot she knew where I lived now and really didn't

wanna invite her in. I also didn't wanna let on that I had my memory back and remembered who she was and every deceitful thing she'd ever done to Shanell and me. I decided to have her stand in the doorway inside the house.

"I was in the middle of eating. Lemme clean my food up real quick, and then we can leave out."

"But why not just stay here and talk?"

"Nah, we can't do that." I went in the kitchen and put my food away and made sure everything was tidy. Spence had just come up from being down in the theater. He noticed Nikki.

"Who da fuck let you in?"

I came walking in the foyer and heard the two of them talking.

"I need to run out for a minute," I said to Spence.

"Alright, let's go." As soon as we all were headed out, Shanell, E, Marcus, and Nevaeh came walking through the door. I was stuck like a muhfucker. Shanell snapped.

"What the fuck is she doing in our house, Jaylen!"

"Baby, I can explain!" Spence, Marcus, and E were just standing around, not knowing what to do. Nevaeh was mad as hell at me, mean mugging me and shit. Momma heard all the commotion and came down the steps. When she saw Nikki and Shanell in my home, I noticed she braced herself. I told Nikki to leave.

"Nikki! Can you please go! We'll talk later!" Her mouth hung open like she had a problem with me telling her to go instead of Shanell.

"Jay, what is she doing here? Shouldn't you be asking her to leave?" she said, looking at Shanell unfavorably.

That set Nevaeh off.

"I know I didn't just hear this bitch say that."

"I got this, Nevaeh," Shanell told her. "Excuse me? You betta get ya ratchet ass out of my house like *he* said!"

Finally, Momma intervened since things seemed to be escalating even more.

"Okay, ladies, that's enough!"

Momma was right. This shit wasn't good at all.

"Nikki you gon' have to go! I'll talk to you later."

She had this crazy look on her face like she was insulted by my words, but she opened the door and walked out but left it wide open.

"Nevaeh," said Marcus. "You mind coming with me to the guest house?"

"You okay, cousin?"

"I will be. You go 'head."

"Ms. Murphy before I go, I just want to apologize for cussing at Nikki in front of you."

"I understand, love, but I appreciate the apology."

E closed the door first, and then he followed behind Marcus and Nevaeh. Spence texted my phone saying he was going back down in the theater where it was safe since it was soundproof. I wanted to laugh, but Shanell would've got in my shit even more, thinking I thought all this was a joke.

"I'm gonna go head back upstairs to let you two sort this out." I hated the way Shanell was staring at me. She was hurt.

The second Momma went up those stairs, Shanell released all her emotions.

"Jay, why?"

"Baby, I swear I didn't know she was coming here."

"Did you tell her where we lived?" I was silent. I knew I did it when I lost my memory. I also remembered everything else that happened with Nikki, and I couldn't even look Shanell in the eyes, so I hung my head low.

"Baby, I'm sorry. I swear I didn't know." I just stopped talking. I knew it was pointless to continue to explain. The tears started to fall as Shanell continued to look at me, even though I couldn't fully look at her, but I saw she was crying. Finally, I held my head up. She continued to have her eyes fixed on me as her tears streamed down her face. I walked a little closer to her to make an attempt to comfort her, but she moved away from me.

"I can't believe you. I've been disappointed with a lot of things that you've done in the past, and you know a lot of it I was able to get past. Especially when it came to Nikki, but this... you hurt me... you've really hurt me. I never would've expected you to have the bitch that's made our lives hell be in our home. I can't stay here anymore."

She turned and walked away from me.

"Shanell, wait!" She kept going and went up to the bedroom with me following right behind her step by step. "I'll leave! Baby, you needa be here."

"How can you expect me to stay here after you had her

here? I feel so violated and disrespected." She continued to grab some things out the drawers.

"Look, you have therapy set up for here, the nurse comes here... I'm the one that fucked up. I'll leave."

"No! This is your house; it's not mine. I'm not your fiancée anymore, so I have no right to stay here. I'll leave."

I grabbed her wrist to stop her movement.

"Shanell, stop being so stubborn all the time. Damn! I'm not letting you leave."

She yanked her hand away from me.

"You should've thought about that before! Oh! And news-flash Jaylen, you have no control over where I can and cannot go!"

"I know that! Baby, I would hate myself if anything happened to you because you left. I needa know that you're gonna be safe, Shanell. Yeah, I was wrong again for not letting you know someone was tryna hurt you and having Nikki in our home, which I honestly had no idea she was coming here. I'm wrong for that, but I'mma make this right, so lemme be the one to leave." She stood there with her thoughts for a minute.

"Jay, what else don't I know about you and Nikki?" I walked in the closet and grabbed a bag then looked at her.

"I'll be outta here in a minute." She noticed I never answered her question. I felt her eyes on me as I gathered some things. I never said another word. She never repeated herself.

I'd been out of the house for a solid week now. I still hadn't made it over to talk to Nikki yet because I needed to calm myself before I had a conversation with her. When I was finally ready to talk to her, I called her up. She had been blowing up my phone anyway, but I wasn't in the mood to talk to her, so I would send it to voicemail. Today, I finally decided to go over there and have this talk that was long overdue. I rang Nikki's doorbell. She answered it and let me in.

"I was in the kitchen sitting at the table filling out some paperwork, so you can follow me back in there."

We both sat at her table, and she went back to writing on the documents she had out. She surprised me being quiet and not her usual doting self. It was refreshing.

"I'mma make this brief. I want you to take a DNA test before the baby's born."

"That's all you have to say to me? No I'm sorry for embarrassing me and being rude to me?"

"Fuck you mean! You showed up at my house uninvited. I don't owe you shit!" She smacked her pen down.

"Like hell you don't! I thought we were working on a relationship again, and then you have her at your house?"

"What? Look, I'm not gon' do this with you, Nikki. I came here to ask you if you could get the DNA test before the baby's born because I needa know this shit now."

"Why? Because of your other baby?" I shook my head, thinking *here she go with the bullshit.*

"Man, what are you talking about?"

"I get it. You think you're gonna find out that this baby isn't yours so you can be free to have your little picture-perfect family with Shanell."

She had me so fucked I sat there wondering why I even came here. I was not in the mood for her nonsense.

"Are you gonna have it done or what?"

"No! I will not lose our baby just so you can be happy that you'll only have one."

That was it. I stood up with both my hands flat on the table as I yelled.

"What you talking 'bout, man! Why would I be happy about the loss of a child? Why would you even say some shit like that?"

I wasn't really paying attention to what Nikki was tryna get at, because I really didn't care. I just wanted to know if she was going to get the DNA test and was waiting to hear a yes.

"You know what? I will get the DNA test just so I can prove to you that this is your baby, and then Shanell will have to accept the fact that you're not the father to only her baby."

"Why you keep talking 'bout another baby? Shanell's not pregnant."

"What? You mean your precious baby didn't tell you that she was expecting?"

"Fuck is wrong witchu? You just make up shit now and spit it like a rapper, huh?"

"She's the one that's lying to you."

"How you know that?"

"Who knows... hmm," she teased, putting her hand on her chin in thought. "Maybe she didn't say anything because it's not yours."

I lifted myself up from the table.

"You got some shit witchu, girl."

"No. Shanell, has some shit with her, but you refuse to see it. She can do no wrong in your eyes."

"Whatever, man... I'mma talk to the doctor and get the DNA test set up. I'm out." I headed toward the door.

"Wait, Jay!" Nikki ran after me. "Don't go! I thought we were gonna pick up where we left off before?" She had me all the way fucked up. "Yeah... that was before. I'll see you at doctor's visits only. Don't you bring yo' ass to my house no more."

My mind was heavy all of a sudden from Nikki saying Shanell was pregnant. I couldn't understand why she would come out and say something like that. Out of all people, I knew Nikki would hate the fact if Shanell was pregnant and it being at the same time as her.

One thing that seemed crazy to me was how happy she was about telling me something that she figured I didn't already know, which made me think it might be true. Especially if it meant Shanell was keeping a secret from me or even lying.

I really had no intentions of going over to the house prior to visiting Nikki, but because of what she said, I needed to talk to Shanell. Spence and I rode over there. I asked E where

Shanell was, and he told me she was up in the bedroom. I walked up the stairs and went in there but still didn't see her. What I did notice was the bathroom door being shut, so I figured maybe she was in there.

I listened closely by the door first to see if I could hear anything. It was quiet, so I opened it. Shanell was laid back with her eyes closed, relaxing, taking a bubble bath. I saw all I needed to see. Shanell jumped because I startled her since she had ear buds in playing music and never heard me enter.

"I don't believe this shit! She actually was telling the truth."

"Shit! Jaylen!" She yelled, grabbing her chest. "You scared me!"

"Yo' ass is fuckin' pregnant?"

She took a breath as she sat up.

"Jay, I wanted to tell you..."

"Is it mine?"

"What?"

"I'm asking you is it mine?"

"Yes! It's yours." She cried. "Why wouldn't it be?"

"Why didn't you tell me?"

"I didn't know how you would feel about it with Nikki being pregnant too." She got out of the tub, and when she did, I just observed her, looking at her bare body. Her stomach was more rounded and formed, unlike before. My mind was gone. In total disbelief. I wanted to be so happy about it, but the fact that she hid it from me had me mad as shit. It was hard to understand why Shanell, out of all people, wouldn't tell me something as wonderful as this. As she tried to wrap up in a towel, I stopped her. I wanted to touch her belly, so I put my hands on it just to confirm that it was real. Shanell's eyes followed.

"You're really pregnant."

Chapter Twelve

SPECIAL DELIVERY

*S*hanell

     "Jay, you gotta know that I was going to tell you. I just wanted to wait until you remembered me... remembered us. I didn't want to overwhelm you with my pregnancy when you already were dealing with the knowledge of possibly being a father to Nikki's baby. You didn't remember me and how much I meant to you... I just thought if you knew—"

Jay moved his hand and angrily interrupted me.

"And if I never get it back, then what would you have done?"

I closed the towel.

"Jay, I wasn't going to keep this from you, I swear. It just would've made it easier to share if you knew the love that you felt for me and how much I meant to you. But you don't. I mean, I know we were starting to connect again, now, but Jay, when I found out I was pregnant you didn't even know who I was. You called off our engagement. I didn't know how to tell you."

"The same way you expect me to tell you shit, Shanell. Just do it! It shouldn't have mattered if I didn't have my memory back. You know me and how important being a father is to me. I would've never turned my back on you, even if I didn't know who you were."

"I'm sorry! I didn't know how to say it... I just needed some time... I wanted to tell when we were in *Fallchester,* but then the moment had gotten away."

He stood there, angered, as he looked toward the floor with his hand resting at his side.

"Yeah, just like I was gonna tell you about El being released but didn't get a chance to before you found out. You gave me hell for that shit."

My eyes squinted at Jay, puzzled.

"How'd you remember that? I never... Jay do you realize what just happened?"

He looked up.

"What?"

"You remembered something else. It just flowed off the top of your head, and you didn't even have to ask me about it. Like you knew what happened."

"Yeah, about that... Shanell, I do know what happened, baby, because I finally got my memory back. I wanted to surprise you and do something special when I told you, but it seems like that ain't gon' get to happen now so..."

My eyes got bigger from the fact that he had his memory again. I was stunned.

"Jay, when?"

"A week ago. When we were sitting in the office."

Once he told me that, my mood changed again.

"You've known since then and didn't even tell me?"

He pointed in my face.

"I know *you* didn't just say that to *me*."

"But, Jay, this is your memory."

"Yeah, just like this is my baby, but it didn't stop you from hiding it, did it?"

"You're right, Jay! I was wrong, okay! Is that what you wanna hear? Let's not forget about how you had me walking around with my life in danger and me not having a clue about that."

"You know what? We can go back and forth on who's right and who's wrong. What difference is it gon' make? We both were wrong."

I walked out of the bathroom, sat on the bed, and broke down even more. My emotions were running high. Jay followed me in the room, but he stood in front of the over-sized window looking straight ahead.

"I never expected any of this to turn out this way. We should be happy about you getting your memory back and my being pregnant, but instead we're fighting." Jay didn't say anything for a few minutes. He just stood over by the window silently with his back turned, looking out of it. I continued to talk. "Everything is just going wrong. Nikki is the devil giving me hell on earth... you probably hate me now... someone is threatening my life. I'm so scared, and I feel so alone. I keep questioning what did I ever do to deserve this. I'm so tired."

Jay

Discreetly, I ran my hand down my face to wipe my tears before I came over to her and took both her hands in mine.

"Stand with me please."

Without any hesitation, she did as I asked. With her hand in mine, I kissed the top of it letting my lips linger for a few. I recognized that in no way was I perfect, and I had also made a lot of mistakes. I realized too, that not only did I put her life in danger but my child's too by not telling her that someone was tryna hurt her. Even though I didn't know she was pregnant, I felt responsible, and it killed me to know that I could've lost not only her, but a child too. As we stood hand in hand, focused in on one another, I gathered myself to speak.

"You know... we've been through a lot of shit. A lotta shit, baby. I'm sorry. I'm so sorry. I would never, ever intentionally put you or our child in danger. You mean..." I started getting choked up. Shanell saw my struggle and wrapped her arms around me and just held me tight. I had to pull myself together so I could finish speaking, because I had a lot I needed to get off my chest. My hands gripped the sides of her arms, pulling her away to look at me.

"First off, I don't want you to ever feel like you deserve any of this shit that's happening to you, and secondly, I could never hate you. I love you. I just love you so much and wanna see you happy that I lose sight of the logical thing to do and end up doing what my heart tells me to do. I know sometimes the heart can be reckless, but that's how I feel when it comes to you, Shanell. I'll do whatever it is I gotta do to keep you safe and to make you happy. Baby, I don't ever want you to feel alone and afraid. I'm here. I know things between us been fucked up lately, and I'm sorry for any and all of my part in it. But, baby, I'm here... again with you... going through a temporary storm that's causing us a lot of turbulence right now. It may last for a little while or the duration of the trip, but I promise you this... we gon' land safely... together." That brought the biggest smile on her face, which in turn made me smile.

Shanell

I missed this part of him and how he knew what to say to make her feel safe and secure like everything was going to be okay.

"Jay, there's something else that I need to tell you, so you might want to keep your seat belt on."

"Why? What is it?"

"Well... baby... we're having twins."

"Twins. Twins? You sure 'bout that?"

"Positive!"

"Damn! I got some powerful shit."

I laughed so hard.

"You are so cocky."

"Aye! You know if I'mma do it I'mma do it big."

"Oh, and one more thing, big head..."

"Aw shit! What?"

"Your babies are due on your birthday." Jay almost picked me up, but he caught himself. Instead, he grabbed my face and kissed me.

"Now that's a birthday gift." Then he pulled me close and wrapped me back in his arms. "You know we got a whole lot of catching up to do, right?"

"Yes, finally! I have been missing my nutty buddy."

Jay went to shut and lock the bedroom door since it had been open. Once he did that, I had him sit down at the foot of the bed. This moment needed some music, so I walked over to the music component in the room and put on some soft sounds. As much as Jay was all over me before, I was surprised to see him patiently sitting there as he watched me.

I dropped my towel and slowly paced myself as I walked in his direction. The soothing sounds coming through the sound system only heightened the mood. As the music played, I began to undress Jay. I wanted to take my time, as I was in no rush. He was worth savoring, and slowly but surely, we were going to make love.

My lips gave his face soft, gentle kisses while I unbuttoned his shirt. Jay was enjoying how I was catering to him, yielding to my affections. I straddled my legs across his lap and let my hands work on his shoulders and rub down his arms as his hand worked on handling my voluptuous ass. Then I kissed different places on his chest and let my tongue trace different spots on his chiseled chest.

Aggressively, I pushed him back on the bed and continued

to kiss on his muscular abs, down to his navel, but it was time to slide everything else off, so I got up and unfastened his belt. I threw his sneakers off one by one, then crawled and sat back on top of him. I feverishly kissed Jay as he embraced me just enough not to put pressure on my mid-section. Before long, I was guiding him inside, ready to partake in a wild ride. I grinded on him nice and slow, clutching my muscles hard, pulling him deep inside of me.

"You love me?" I asked at a whisper.

Jay was so caught up in the moment he could barely say it back. I knew I was getting the best of him and speeded up my thrusts just a touch. Jay was palming my ass, slamming my love cove down on his dick as he stroked back to no end.

His pounding was beginning to be a bit much as he hit my hot spot again and again, making me cum. I had exhausted a lot of my energy, but I knew my baby still needed to release. Since Jay loved to hit it from the back, I laid on my side. He positioned himself behind me, lifted my leg, and went in.

With his other hand rubbing my love cove just a taste, he worked his way to a climax and me into another. With bodies intertwined and dripping wet Jay released my leg and fell back on the bed coming down from his high. After a few moments, he lovingly kissed my cheek then snuggled up behind me and held me in his arms.

"I love you, baby," he stated as his face rested lightly on my cheek. I laid there with a smile. I was so happy that he finally knew about the pregnancy and his memory was back.

Everything was finally out in the open, and now we could finally move on with no more secrets.

———————

Two months had passed, and Jay and I had really been trying to get back on track. Nevaeh was still in *Velport*. Marcus talked her into staying as a precaution in case she was a target. She honestly didn't think anyone was trying to come after her, but she decided to stay a little longer. She already had a relative at her house keeping an eye on things, so she extended her stay.

Since Jay finally had his memory back, Lyric decided to go home. She knew we needed our time, and she also thought it was best for her own good. She was slapped with a restraining order from Nikki, and if she didn't get away from her, she was going to kill her. She was so psyched to hear that we were having twins. She told Jay we should consider naming one of the babies after her if it was girls.

His mom was excited too. She already was talking about taking care of the expenses for the nursery. She told me anything that we wanted to do, was on her. I was so relieved that his mom didn't hold it against me for not letting her know right away about the pregnancy. She told me she didn't like the fact that I kept it from Jay and her, but that was in the past, and we were moving forward.

Jay's protective nature had just been magnified now with my pregnancy. It was understandable, too, since we still didn't know who had been posing as a threat to me. The cops were still investigating with no real leads since Jay's fan club was enormous, and the ones that were suspects had alibis. With that, Jay felt the need to be close by. He still had promoting to do for the video, but after that was done, he wasn't scheduling anything.

I was finally done with physical therapy and at the end of my stint with needing a visiting nurse. The babies were developing as they should with the morphine not being an issue, but now there were new concerns. My cervix had started to dilate. This was too early. I was just about seven months. I was in the hospital for a few days and had to be placed on strict bed rest.

The doctor said I needed to be in a stress-free environment, or I would be put back in the hospital for the duration of my pregnancy. Jay decided to pay for me to have my own private nurse. We really liked Kelli, so he worked out an arrangement where she could care for me also at home. Jay knew too that we had a good rapport, so anything to keep me in good spirits for the duration, he was all for.

Jay also kept up with going to doctor's visits with Nikki. I didn't like it of course, but I understood his need to do so. They did find out that Nikki was having a baby girl through ultrasound. He finally told me that one day when I had asked. He never spoke about Nikki to me because he didn't want to make me feel any stress, but I asked, so he told me. The thought of her possibly carrying my fiancé's child was hard to wrap my head around, and I hoped I didn't have to.

Jay

Today, I had it penciled in to go with Nikki to get the results of the DNA test that we finally went and had done. I was going alone. Not even Spence was accompanying me. Shanell had no idea today was the day I would officially know. I just wanted to wait until I heard the results and then tell her at that time. Once I arrived at the hospital, I went to the waiting area on the floor that I was meeting Nikki on. I made sure to dress in layers with a hoody on and some shades to not draw much attention. I noticed Nikki was already here. I could tell she was nervous. I was too. I just wanted this to be over, and I would officially know if I was the father or not.

Suddenly, we were called to go in the doctor's office.

"Hello, Nikki... Jay."

We both spoke at the same time.

"Hi, Dr. Gibson."

"Hello."

"So are you guys ready to hear what these results are?"

Shit, I'd been ready since she first claimed this shit, but I kept my response cool.

"Most definitely."

Nikki briefly stared at me before answering.

"Yes. We're ready."

Dr. Gibson opened the file.

"Okay, well it says here that, Jay, you are 99.999 percent the father." Nikki looked at me with the biggest grin on her face. I had no expression, but that was all I needed to know. I wasn't too happy about having to go home and tell Shanell the results, but at least all the doubt could be removed.

"Well, if you guys have no questions or concerns about anything, I'll see you in a few weeks."

We got up and walked out of the office. Nikki got her appointment for her next visit, and then we left out.

"Jay, can you walk with me to my floor? I gotta go back to work." I was still walking with thoughts of Shanell on my mind as Nikki was talking.

"I can't, Nikki. I gotta go."

"Jay, wait!" She stood in front of me to stop me. "I just wanna say I really appreciate how kind you've been to me, even though I know you're only doing it because of the baby. But I hope now that you know she's really yours, we can genuinely work on being friends again. We got a baby to be parents to, you know."

"Nikki, you think just like that I'm gonna forget everything that you've done to me and Shanell? I might've had amnesia and forgot for a period of time, but that's all over with. I'd be a fool to let you raise my daughter. Like I said before, enjoy your nine months. My baby girl's coming with me." I walked away from her, but she ran up from behind and grabbed my arm.

"Wait a minute! How could you even think about separating a baby from its mother. She's my baby too!"

"That you wanted with me! Now, you got it. I'm fighting for custody. Now I can get what I want." I walked away again, but she just yelled after me as I approached the elevators.

"I hate you!" The elevator doors opened, and I got on them alone. Once I got home, I was looking for Shanell. I noticed Kelli was at the house, but Shanell wasn't.

"Aye. Where she at?"

"I found a note on the board in the kitchen saying she needed to go over to her job real quick and she'd be right back."

"She know she ain't s'posed to be going nowhere."

"She's been real good about being on bed rest, so this one time shouldn't hurt anything."

"Alright, well I got a meeting to go to. You gon' be alright here if I go?"

"Oh, sure I'll be fine. I'll wait around until Shanell gets back."

"Thank you, Kelli, for everything."

"You're welcome."

Kelli

I went in the kitchen after Jay left to check and see if Shanell had been taking her vitamins as prescribed. I used to watch her take them with her breakfast sometimes since Shanell hated to do it. She promised me that she would continue to take them and not miss any days. When I opened the pill bottle, I noticed the pills that were in there weren't her vitamins. I had an idea of what they could've been but wasn't for certain, so I decided to investigate it more once Shanell had gotten back.

Shanell

Everyone was so excited to see me at the job. It had been so long since I really got to talk to any of them. Lynn was rubbing on my belly as she congratulated me about the twins.

"I knew I saw babies in you guys' future."

"You jinxed us."

"Please! The way you two are always all over each other, it was bound to happen."

"How's your family, especially your little one?"

"Oh, she's getting so big. I'm warning you now, they don't stay babies for long. Although, in your case, having to deal with two, you might be happy about that." I laughed. Then Val came in the building. She was on lunch when I arrived.

"Oh my gosh! Look at you!" She gave me a hug.

"Hello, Valerie. It's good to see you."

"Girl, I'm so happy that you're gonna be alright. My uncle did an awesome job on your scar too."

"Oh, yeah, that's right," added Lynn. "I forgot you even had it concealed."

"Oh, yeah, before I forget, Shanell, this was dropped off up here for you." Val handed me a big yellow envelope with no return address on it.

"What is this?"

"I don't know. My cousin came up here to have lunch with me and said she saw it on the floor and gave it to me. Maybe the postman dropped it by accident."

Lynn had her head in the air looking at it trying to read it.

"Well, you would think he would notice that. It's not like it's a small envelope."

"Well, I better get home. I know I'm supposed to be on bed rest, but I needed to get out of the house. Plus, I needed to pick up some more things from my desk."

"You know Jay could've come up here for you."

"You're not happy to see me, Lynn?"

"Of course, but you really should be off your feet."

"How far along are you now, Shanell?" asked Val.

"Just turned seven months."

"You're huge, girl. Wow!"

"I know! I'm going to need a personal trainer to get back into shape."

"Well, let me know if you're serious. I can recommend one," she said.

"Um thanks, but no thanks." Val squinted her eyes at me, now looking irritated.

"I'm not gonna even go there, but my uncle is innocent. That's all I'm saying."

"Well on that note, I'm out of here." I was escorted out with Evan and Marcus by my side. Once I got home, I noticed Kelli was there. "I tried to get here as soon as I could."

"No, you're fine. Hey, listen. These pills right here—" I interrupted her and took the bottle.

"You would be proud. I've been taking them faithfully."

"And I commend you for that, but I called your doctor, and he wants you to stop taking these."

"Why?"

"Don't worry he just wants to give you a new prescription."

"Kelli, be honest with me, is there a problem? I mean, why does he want to give me something new?"

"Shanell, relax. I'm going to check your vitals and then I need to go back to the hospital to check on your prescription. Everything will be fine."

"I don't understand why he wants to change it though. Is this something that can hurt my babies?"

"Shanell, I can't give you any answers right now because I'm not the doctor. All I know is your doctor wants you to stop taking these particular ones. Now where are you going to relax at, down here or in your room?"

"I'll be up in the bedroom."

Kellie checked me out and then she headed over to the hospital. I decided to see what was in the yellow envelope that Val handed to me. When I opened it, it was a DVD. I thought it was strange for someone to send a DVD for me to watch to my job, but I put it in. When it started, Jay was walking over to none other than Autumn and taking his clothes off.

I watched the rest of it, emotionless. I couldn't even feel the knife that was suddenly stabbed in my heart. The only thing I could feel was the man in that video not being the person I thought I knew at all. I quickly grabbed my suitcases and started packing as much as I could. Once I was finished, I called Marcus and Evan to come upstairs. They looked at me like I was crazy, especially Marcus who always was more vocal than Evan.

"Where you going?"

I looked at Evan, not even bothering to respond to Marcus.

"Can you guys put these in the car and take me to the condo?"

"Shanell, I don't think you staying there is—"

"Not right now, Evan! I'm not interested in your thoughts! Just do what I said and take me over there!"

"Okay, Shanell. Be cool. I hear you," he responded.

I could tell Marcus really wanted to know what happened. He kept looking at the opened yellow envelope I had on the bed. He didn't say anything though. He just picked up what was left of my suitcases and walked down to the car.

Jay

When I finally came home, I looked around the house for Shanell. I saw Spence in the theater, and he obviously could see I was back.

"You see Shanell?"

"Last time I saw her she was upstairs with Marcus and E. They left?"

"I think so. I'm 'bout to call her."

When I tried, it went straight to voicemail, so I called Marcus.

"Yo, where y'all at?"

"She wanted to come to the condo."

"Can you put her on the phone? I keep getting her machine."

I heard Marcus tell Shanell I was on the phone.

"I don't wanna talk to him, Marcus!" She yelled in the background.

"Look, Shanell, I ain't getting caught in the middle of this. You don't wanna talk to him, you tell him." She finally took it because she yelled in my ear the minute she got it.

"You lyin', cheatin' ass! Leave me the fuck alone!"

Then she hung up. I was lost. I called Marcus back.

"Yo! What the fuck's going on? What's wrong with her?"

"Nigga, I wish I could tell you. All I know is you might wanna check what was in that yellow envelope she got from work that's up in y'all's bedroom. It seems like she got upset after she opened that."

I hung up with Marcus and walked up to the bedroom. There it was, the envelope he mentioned, on the bed, but it was empty. My eyes searched the room to see if I could find any clues as to what was in it. Then I noticed the light on from the DVD player. Skeptical about watching whatever this was, I turned on the TV and hit play with the remote to see if it was what got Shanell so upset.

My eyes grew ten times in size once I saw my fucking session with Autumn had been recorded. Instantly, I dropped the remote and paced the floor frantically with my hands on my head about to lose my fuckin' mind. She knew. I couldn't believe Autumn did this shit to me, and now Shanell knew about it.

That encounter, I had planned on taking to the grave. I sat on the bed with my head in my hands for a second. I wanted to fuck some ass up. Some Autumn ass! It was no need in sitting around moping, so Spence and I left out the house to go over to the condo. I knocked on the door first to see if Shanell would let me in.

"Go away, Jay!"

Since that wasn't going to work, I decided to use the key. She must've forgot I had a key, because the moment I walked in, her mouth was hanging open, staring at my hand. Marcus, E, and Spence decided to leave us alone to talk. I stared at Nevaeh, wondering if she was going to follow suit. She looked at Shanell first, like she wanted her approval before being dismissed.

"It's okay. I'll be fine."

She walked out, leaving us alone. I shut the door behind her, only to find Shanell standing right there, not allowing me to go any further.

"Why are you here!"

I noticed the way she stood with her arms folded, all closed off, before anything was even said. The way she looked at me was chilling.

"Baby, can I please explain to you *that* situation?"

"Hell no!" she roared. "There is nothing you can say to me that I couldn't see for myself. The bottom line is you fucked her. I don't care how it went down or even why it went down, but you did it. Freely! I hope she was worth it."

"Look, I know you don't wanna hear I'm sorry, so I'm not

even gonna insult you with saying that. I mean, that whole situation wasn't—"

"Jaylen, do you honestly think I wanna hear anything you have to say about this?" she yelled, flailing her hands as she stressed her emotions. Her anger then led her to get up in my face. "You had your dick up in that bitch! You had your lips kissing on her and your hands touching her. I can't even get the sight of you fucking her out of my head!"

She turned her back and walked away.

"That ain't mean shit to me!"

She stopped walking and turned back around.

"Hell! I guess I didn't either. You did it the day after you told me you wanted to give us a chance. How dare you!"

I stepped over to her, tryna get her to believe me.

"And I do!"

I reached for her hands.

"Don't touch me!" All I could do was stare at her for a second. I saw another woman standing in front of me. She was callous and hardhearted. This was a different Shanell. I felt her wrath and knew I really fucked up this time. "You know... I really can't afford to be arguing with you, Jay, and getting upset like this."

"Baby, I know, and I'm not tryna—"

"No! Listen to me, Jay! I need for you to leave."

"Shanell, baby, just lemme talk to you," I begged.

"Please, Jay! Just leave! If you ever cared about me, just go... please..." She cried. "I can't do this anymore."

"Fuck that! This is all bullshit! But I hear what you saying, and for right now, I'll go, but this ain't over. You know me well enough to know it's far from being over."

I was so frustrated with all the bullshit. I was tired of people trying to come in between my happiness. I wasn't letting Shanell go without a fight and was making it my business to get to the bottom of my recorded encounter. I left with Spence and tried calling Autumn on the way to the car. She wasn't answering. That made me decide to go over to Shanell's job and find out more about the envelope that was dropped off, but first, I had to go by the house to get it.

Val was bringing a call to an end as I stood in front of the desk waiting. Seeing her only brought back the memory of my pushing up on her in the club. All I needed was Shanell to find out about that shit too. I had to play this cool.

"Hey, Jay! How's my girl doing?"

"She's good. Look, Val, can you tell me anything about this envelope that was brought here?"

I showed it to her.

"Oh, yeah. My cousin brought that in here. She said the mailman must've dropped it by accident."

"But if you notice, this isn't even post marked. Someone had to personally bring it here."

She took another look.

"Oh! You're right. I didn't even notice that."

"Who's your cousin?"

"Her name is Autumn. You should know her. She was in your video."

"Wait! She's ya cousin?"

"Yeah."

"Small world. I do know her. I've been tryna get in touch with her so she could be compensated from the video matter of fact. They don't have the correct address."

"Oh! Here, I'll give it to you."

Valerie wrote it down and gave it to me. That was my next stop.

"Thanks! For everything," I said, grabbing her hands and carefully eyeing her, hoping she caught my drift.

"No problem! It's all good."

We headed to Autumn's residence, but some other chick answered the door.

"Aye! Is Autumn here?"

"Well. Well. Well. If it isn't Jay Murphy. Come in, why don't ya."

Spence walked in ahead of me to check the place out.

"Is she here?"

"No. She's out with her homey. Do you need me to give her a message for you?"

"Nah, I just really needed to talk to her. She has something that belongs to me."

"Well, her room is right over there if you wanna go see if it's in there."

Spence and I looked at each other at the same time. I was wondering if this girl was fo' real.

"You just gon' let me go in her room like that?"

"Why should I care? She's a bitch!"

"Who are you?"

"Excuse my manners. I'm her sister Summer."

"You not gon' snitch if I do this, are you?"

"Aye, I live here too. Be my guest," she said, unbothered.

"Where's her room at?"

"Follow me."

She led us to Autumn's room. It was very clean and neatly organized. I didn't know if I would find a copy of the DVD or even the original. Shit, I didn't even know where to begin to look or exactly what to look for. I just knew I needed some answers.

"Oh, and she hides stuff in her mattress, so you might wanna check there too."

I was tripping. What was it with this girl? I couldn't believe she was dogging her sister out like this to help me. I checked underneath her mattress and stumbled across her journal and briefly skimmed over a few pages. The few things I saw were X-rated.

"Just what the fuck I can use."

I was gon' hold onto this shit and use it as leverage in case I didn't find what I came for. Spence was checking in her bathroom.

"Yo, man, check this out." I went in there. Spence had her medicine cabinet open and noticed some unopened syringes. "What the fuck's up with this shit?"

"I don't know." I called Summer in the room. "Aye, by any chance is ya sister a diabetic?"

"No."

"Is she sick?"

"No! Why'd you think that?" I didn't know if I should say why, in case her sister didn't know shit, but she started talking again before I could respond, anyway. "If you've come across some medical supplies, she steals them from my dad's office."

"Oh, ya dad's some type of doctor?"

"Yeah, so sorry to disappoint you, but she's totally fake. Well, at least her lips are. She gets collagen injections... I know you didn't think she was a natural beauty." I laughed. Crazy as it seemed, I was really getting a kick out of Summer. I liked her flow, but for her to be Autumn's sister, she was going in on her hard.

"Yo, man, why you got it in for ya sister like that?"

"She's a crazy bitch! You don't have to live with her."

"So won't you move out?"

"I would, but I'm having so much fun blackmailing her being here."

That raised my eyebrows as I looked at Spence.

"Did she just say she blackmailing her sister?"

"That's what the fuck I heard."

"Damn! What type of shit is—" I caught myself. I didn't wanna judge. "Okay, baby. I appreciate all your help, but we better go. Maybe I'll give you some tickets and backstage passes or something to one of my shows. 'Preciate ya time though."

"No offense, but I'm not a fan." Spence started cracking up. I let out a chuckle as well. Wasn't expecting that.

"Nah, she keeping it real. I like that. Well, what else can I do for you then?"

"Now, if you can get me backstage to see Naeema, we can call it even."

"It's a done deal. Gimme ya number." She gave me her info. "Don't let her find out I was here, especially with all that blackmailing shit y'all got going on. That ain't cool."

"It ain't like she's never done it to me before, so payback is a bitch."

"So what you getting out of it?"

"I don't have to pay any bills and get to live here rent free, so I'll deal with her royal bitchiness for that."

"Well, good luck with whatever you tryna do. Thanks again for the help." Then I thought about her tryna do that shit to me. "Hold up! I don't have to worry about being black-mailed, do I...? This all seems kinda suspect, you being so helpful and shit."

She laughed like what I said was the funniest thing.

"I may not be a fan of your music, but *you* I like, so you're safe."

"Alright! I got a witness. You try to lie later and shit, I'mma—"

"Jay! It's all good! I promise you."

I'mma be in touch about those passes once I see when she performing again."

"I already know that info, but I'll let you do your home-work. You have the number."

She walked us to the door, and we left out. On our way to the house, I was skimming Autumn's journal while talking to

Spence. "Damn! I see my name on almost every page in this bitch."

"What the fuck you be doing to these girls, man?"

I glanced at another page.

"She got some crazy shit in here. Her freaky ass a trip. I can't wait 'til I see this bitch."

Chapter Thirteen

BITTER

utumn

"You are the fuckin' devil! I swear!"

I was going back and forth between my dressers and my suitcase, packing to get away for a while as I yelled at my sister.

"Me! You hoe ass bitch! I'm tired of saving your ass! You brought this shit on yourself."

"You didn't have to let him in here. That shit was foul, even for you. Now he has my journal. You've ruined everything!"

"I had no idea he would find that or even take it. Shit! I didn't even know where you kept it."

"Stop lying, Summer! Then again, that always was your problem."

"What difference does it make if he has your journal? You have him being recorded. What could be worse than that?"

I stared hard at my clueless ass sister. How could she not understand that my innermost thoughts and encounters that I'd had were in there. My secrets. They were not my own anymore if he'd read it. She fuckin' screwed me. I zipped up my suitcase.

"You wouldn't begin to understand."

"It isn't my fault that you recorded y'all having sex and now he's after you. What the fuck you expect was gonna happen once he knew?"

"Go fuck off, Summer! I see the less you know, the better."

I dragged my suitcase out the room. Summer followed behind me.

"I hope you don't expect me to keep up with your bills. I'm not paying for shit while you're gone," she griped, stopping by the door with her arms folded.

"You know what? You've done enough already. Believe me! I don't need you doing shit for me." I got in her face. "Remember that! Just know I'm going away for a while, and don't bother asking where, because I'm not telling you."

"I don't care where you go, Autumn. I'll actually get a vacation now."

"You little shit," I scolded, pointing in her face. "It's going to come a day when I won't care what you have on me, and then you won't have anything to hold over me anymore. You wait and see."

"Welp! Today's not that day!" She went to open the door. "Bye, bitch!"

I looked at her with pure hate.

"Kiss my ass, Summer! Goodbye, and take care of my fuckin' house!" I yelled as I walked to my car.

She waved at me in the doorway.

"Adios!"

Shanell

Jay was still out of the house. I was through and didn't want anything to do with him. We were like strangers again, and when he told me about the baby, I barely was able to let him confirm it. Another blow that I honestly wasn't handling very well.

When he came along with me on doctor's visits, I had nothing to say. I was over seven months pregnant now and still under strict bed rest orders. Unfortunately, that discovery Kelli made was another attempt to hurt me. Someone had switched the pills that should've been in my vitamin bottle, with over-the-counter herb vitamins that had Barberry in them, which is an herb that contains high levels of berberine, known to stimulate uterine contractions.

For whatever reason, they were trying to make me go into

labor prematurely. If taken over a period of time, I very well could've had complications. Luckily, I hadn't been taking them for long, but my doctor believed that was why I'd started dilating. Now anytime anyone wrote a prescription for me or saw me, they had to leave their fingerprint on the paperwork so they would have a more traceable paper trail.

We did find out a while back that we were having a boy and a girl. It had been so much going on that I really hadn't had time to absorb everything yet. Jay admitted at one of the appointments he thought if he gave me some time, eventually I would come around and at least talk to him about how I felt about things. If it wasn't pertaining to the twins, I had nothing to say. That! We both were very excited about and discussed with ease. He asked me if I thought about any names. I told him I'd been toying with a few ideas. He would try to ease into another conversation afterwards, not involving the twins, but it never worked.

As hard as he would try to get me to talk or go somewhere where we could be alone, I wasn't budging. I was hurting so badly, but only Nevaeh and Kelli knew my real pain. I continuously cried. Kelli constantly had to remind me to try to keep it together for the sake of my babies, but it was so hard. Jay was my heart, and when he broke it, he left me broken inside and very bitter.

Jay

These past few weeks hadn't been easy in the least. I couldn't catch up with Autumn's ass, and Nikki kept fuckin' around changing her doctor's visits so I couldn't go, which was pissing me the fuck off. Then there was Shanell. I was fuckin' lost without her. All I could do around her was talk about the babies. She wasn't hearing shit else I had to say. I just poured that shit into my writing.

Kyle and I were working on a few songs that I felt real good about. One day when we were brainstorming the hook for one of 'em, I got a call from Charmaine.

"Jay! I'm so glad you answered."

"Who's this?"

"It's Charmaine. I have Nikki's phone. I need you to get over to the hospital."

"Is she in labor?"

"Just get here!"

She gave me all the info, and Spence and I went over there. I was hoping she wasn't going into labor yet, because it would've been a bit early. Once I got there, I saw Charmaine. She was crying. I ran over to her.

"What happened?"

"I don't know! She just started bleeding!" My heart was beating fast from the unknown. All I could do was pray that her and my baby girl were going to be alright. I waited for hours in a private room with Charmaine. Finally, the doctor came in there to talk to us.

"Are you dad?"

"Yes sir. I am... Are they alright? Just tell me they're alright." I tried to read his eyes to see if they would give away anything, but it all seemed grim.

"I'm afraid I have some good news and bad news." I turned my back on the doctor. For the first time, I was afraid of what I was about to hear. I braced myself and then turned back around to hear the news.

"What's goin' on, Doc?"

I blew in my hands as I held them in a praying position in front of my lips.

"It seems Nikki has suffered from a condition we call Placental Abruption. It's when the placenta, the organ that nourishes the fetus, separates from its attachment to the uterine wall, before the baby is born."

The thumping of my heart only got louder in my ears.

"So what are you saying? She had to deliver her early?"

"We did have to go in and get the baby out, but... unfortunately, we couldn't get her to breathe." My eyes widened.

"Nah, man... nooo..." I debated, shaking my head in disbelief. "Nooo... my baby girls not..."

Charmaine cried out too.

"No! Not the baby!"

"I'm sorry." Instantly, I fell apart. "I'm so sorry for your loss. I really wish I had better news to give you. We did everything we could to bring her back. She just wasn't strong enough."

I moved away from the two of them to be in my own space for a minute. My mood was somber. My heart was crushed. I wiped my face and turned toward the doctor's direction again. I looked at him with a heavy heart.

"You couldn't save my baby, man?"

I know what was said, but I was full of hope like I was going to hear a different response.

"This is never something that's easy to tell a parent. We really did do everything that we possibly could've... On a more positive note, Nikki is stable now. She had some hemorrhaging, but we were finally able to stop the bleeding. It was just too much for..."

I couldn't hear no more and stormed out the room. I was devastated. There was only one place to go, so I walked to the hospital chapel for guidance. As soon as I made it to the front, it was like I couldn't hold my own any longer and just dropped to my knees and wept uncontrollably. I couldn't understand why this little bundle that I saw on ultrasounds and had listened to the heartbeat had been taken away.

Even though I never met her, I loved her. She was my little angel. It pained me to know that she would never get to know me, and I her. Then I started thinking about that DNA test and if that had anything to do with it. I thought maybe if I'd waited, this would've never happened. Maybe that was what caused her condition. The thought of that upset me even more, and at that moment, I blamed myself. Once I calmed down, I lit a candle for her, said a prayer, and got my mind together to go see Nikki. I knew this was *not* going to be easy.

When I got to the room, Charmaine was sitting by Nikki's side as she laid there. She got up and left out so we could be alone. It was hard seeing the fragile state she was in. I'd never seen her this powerless. She was just lying there with a vacant look, staring off in space. She looked sleep deprived from crying so much. Once I sat down beside her, she sat up and grabbed tightly on to me. She needed to be comforted, and so did I as both our worlds were shattered in pieces. We held each other and mourned the loss of our little girl together.

"So uh... did you... did you at least get to see her?"

She continued to sob as she answered.

"I saw her, Jay. I saw our baby... she was so beautiful and tiny. Her little hands and feet just laid there, lifeless... Why'd our baby have to die, Jay... why?"

That was one question I wished I had the answer to, but I didn't. I just hugged Nikki.

"I wish that wasn't even a question right now."

She suddenly let me go and looked at me with a tightness in her eyes. Her emotions changed. "This is all your fault! You only wanted Shanell's baby! You never really wanted me to be pregnant anyway! You didn't want her! You just wanted to punish me! Well I'm being punished, okay!"

"Nikki, that's not true."

"Yes, it is! You wanted our baby to die. Well are you happy now!"

I knew Nikki was hurting, so I tried to let her words roll off, but in the back of my mind, I did blame himself. She was so quick to dismiss my pain and not see that I was torn up inside too. The nurse came in the room since she heard Nikki hollering.

"Is everything okay, Ms. Williams?"

"No! I want him out of here!"

Since I didn't wanna upset her any further, I left.

I wanted to have a proper burial for our daughter Angel Nicole Williams. It was a private ceremony and very intimate. That was a rough day for us both, but somehow, we made it through it. Shanell had heard about what happened from Kelli. She did call me, but at the time, she got my voicemail and just left me a message. I didn't give her a call until two weeks later. I really needed some time to regroup and reflect on a lot of things.

When I did finally call her back, I asked her if we could talk. Even though she knew she was on strict bedrest, she still agreed to see me. I told E to bring her where I was staying, which was at the *Noble Garden Hotel,* so he drove her over.

"I'll give you a call when I'm ready for her to leave."

"Got it."

As soon as the door was shut and we were alone, we embraced. We stayed in that same spot for a few, just holding one another. Then I took Shanell by the hand so she could have a seat and get off her feet, and I sat down beside her. She really was filling out. It was good to see life still growing.

"Jay, I'm really sorry about the baby."

"I appreciate that, baby."

"You know I would've been there, but out of respect to Nikki I didn't think I should come. I did call you. Did you get my messages?"

I showed a glimpse of a smile, partially because I knew how sincere she was being.

"Baby, it's okay. I knew you would've come. I wouldn't have wanted you there anyway, truthfully. It's cool though."

"How are you holding up?"

I sighed heavily.

"It's tough, man. I still can't believe she's gone. I be picturing what she would've looked like since I never saw her... if she would've had mine or my momma's smile. What her personality would've been like... a whole bunch of shit." I rubbed my hand down my chin, as just talking about her in the past tense still seemed unreal. Then I cleared my throat since I could feel myself getting choked up. "But uh, I know God had a reason for taking her, you know. I know she's in a better place than here... I just wish she was," I confessed. Shanell lightly put her hands on the sides of my face, grabbing my attention like she used to. I knew pain was plastered all over it. As our eyes met, a tear fell.

"Baby, I'm so sorry." She wiped it away. I didn't wanna start getting upset again, so I changed the subject as I changed my positioning on the sofa.

"... Anyway, what's been going on with you, my soldier and my princess. Everything still alright?" I felt all on Shanell's belly, lightening the mood. Then I lifted her top and kissed it cherishing what had yet to come. As soon as I did, one of 'em moved. I jerked my head back, amazed. "You feel that?"

"Of course. I feel them all the time. I think they be fighting for space."

That was a laugh I could've used in that moment.

"This shit's incredible."

Then I started talking to her stomach.

"I've missed nights when you would do that."

I felt more movement as my hands palmed her stomach like a beach ball.

"Ow!"

"I bet you that was Jay Jr."

"We never discussed a boy having your name," she said jokingly.

"I know, but for now, I'm just calling him Jay Jr. since we haven't decided on a name yet."

"Then Jay Jr. just hurt me if it was him. He must not be too happy right now."

"Neither is his father," I admitted as my eyes slowly met up with Shanell's. "I miss you... I know I messed up real bad, Shanell. I been doing a lot of thinking, and I don't want this to be over. I love you. I don't know how to stop."

"Jay, to be honest with you, I'm still confused, and I really need some answers."

"Anything!"

I sat up to give her my full attention.

Shanell

"Well, Jay, if you really want us to talk, I need to know a few things, and I need for you to be honest about it."

"Whatever you wanna know."

"How did you come to know Autumn?"

"I've known of her for a while. She's usually at my shows and always hanging around backstage and at afterparties. It wasn't until this last tour that we started talking more than usual."

I wasn't sure if I was prepared to hear anymore.

"You know what? I thought I wanted to know this, but suddenly, I'm not so sure."

"I need to tell you this. When I say talking, I mean just that. Having regular conversations. It was completely innocent. Then I guess when you went in that coma and I knew it would be a while before I could see you, that fucked with me a lot. She would be around sometimes since she had access backstage, and I guess she noticed it. It was hard not to, I'm sure. That was a rough time for me, Shanell. Then it got to a point when I would see her, she would always ask about you and wanna talk about you. I needed that. It was an outlet for me."

"So was that your only time sleeping with her?"

"I've never slept with her before that day. What you saw was it."

"So were you going to tell me about you sleeping with her, Jay?"

"Why would I tell you something like that? I never meant for it to happen."

"Gee! Thanks for being honest, now!"

"Shanell, you don't know how bad I wish I could take that moment back. I didn't have my memory at that time, and I'm not tryna make no excuses for it... I just know if things were different, I wouldn't have slept with her. I loved you, which was why I never let that shit happen before, except for when it happened with Nikki, and you know I was drugged."

"I guess we'll never know, will we?"

"I wouldn't have."

"That's something else I don't get. I've never known for you to be clumsy. Jay how'd that happen... the accident? How'd you fall?"

"Man, that shit was crazy... Look, this what happened. I had just finished performing a song with Acqwon and was going to get my things so I could get to you. I was going down the steps, and the next thing I knew, I was waking up in the hospital."

"I had no idea you knew her for some time. I always thought I could trust you while you were away."

"Baby, you can trust me. I know it may not seem like it right now, but you can. I'll do whatever I gotta do to earn that back. I just don't want you to give up on us like that." Suddenly, Spence came to Jay's door. I heard him say to Jay once he answered it, they needed him to come down to the front desk for a minute.

"I'll be right back. We not finished talking, so don't try to leave."

"Go on. I'll be here. Don't forget you have to call Evan first anyway."

"Don't answer this door for nobody. I'll be right back."

I waved him off.

Jay

Spence and I headed down to the front desk. Apparently,

someone had damaged my truck in the garage. They asses flattened all my tires I was told. This was Spence's first time hearing this too, because they would only disclose the information to me. That made me nervous about leaving Shanell up in the room by herself.

"Yo, man, I wanna go back and be with Shanell. You go 'head and handle the rest of this."

"I think I should accompany you back up there, just in case whoever did it is still around."

"I'm good!"

Spence just saw me to the elevators and then went back over to the desk. When I walked in, immediately, I didn't see Shanell.

"Shanell!"

I ran to see if she was in the bathroom. Nothing. Panic began to set in. I didn't want to think about what could've happened, but my gut was telling me I knew. Then Spence came in as I was on my way to the door.

"Where's Shanell? She in here?"

"Man, she not in here, Spence... She's not here, man!"

"Damn! Okay, listen, man, we got us a situation... this time, El escaped. I was just down there talking to the police, and they said he was about to be transported to a new facility and somehow made a thorough escape. They think he had help."

"Clash!"

That was the sound of a vase I threw, shattering as it hit the wall. Somebody was fucking with my family for far too long. I'd had enough. I was ready to kill a muhfucker on the spot, and if this had something to do with him, he definitely was a dead man this time.

Shanell

When I woke up, I had no idea where I was and why I had this throbbing headache. My mouth was taped shut, and my hands were tied to the bed. I couldn't see anyone in sight either, because they had a blindfold on me. Wherever I was, it was very quiet. I tried to make noise, but the sound was so muffled, I realized it was no use.

Finally, someone came and removed the blindfold. It was Autumn. Then everything started coming back to me about being at the hotel with Jay.

Knock! Knock! Knock!

"Room service."

I knew Jay said not to answer, but he must've forgotten he ordered room service. I was sure he'd want me to get his food, so I got up to get it. It was a nun. I found it odd that she said room service not in a hotel uniform or with any food. I smiled at first.

"I'm sor—" She pulled me out into the hallway, taking me by surprise. "What are you—" I felt and heard a clicking sound as the object was forced into my back. That silenced me real quick, reducing my next words to a sigh.

"I'm going to need you to walk out of here quietly and like your life depended on it, because it does."

Someone else was behind me. My first thoughts were for my babies because I didn't want any harm to come to them. I constantly took in deep breaths to control my breathing for their sakes, because a panic attack was on the verge.

"I'll do... whatever you want. I... I promise. Please just... don't hurt me."

We walked out of there, me be being as normal as possible not to raise any suspicions. Then once we got to the car, they put a cloth up to my face, and that's the last thing I remembered.

"Surprised to see me? I see you went and got knocked up by my man. Humph! Wasn't expecting that! It would be just like you to think a baby is going to keep a man like that. Got ya face all prettied up just for a wedding day that you won't get to see. Didn't think I knew that, huh!" she jeered while shaking her head in my face.

Autumn took the tape off my lips and tried to force hers to mine right after. I screamed as I turned my face and pushed her mouth away using it. She laughed uncontrollably, like it was a joke. I couldn't believe this nightmare I was living, again. "You can scream all you want. I'd doubt if anyone hears you." I was so confused as to why she would do this to me.

"I don't understand. I don't even know you. What could you possibly want with me, Autumn?"

"What do I want?" she asked, pointing to herself. "It's simple. I want Jay! You know... he wanted me too," she raved while her eyes went up, and she batted her lashes as she smiled. "You don't know how long I wanted him to fuck me."

She put her hands on the bed and leaned into my face again. "It was gooood," she sang. "But you know that. You saw it, right?" She whispered, carefully mouthing her words in my face, "I can still feel his lips on my body. I watch it when I need an orgasm. Mmm." Then she rolled her tongue over her top lip.

I wanted to spit in her face.

"I'm done with Jay... You can have him! Just let me go!" I fussed.

"You ain't going nowhere, bitch! But I'mma take real good care of you. I just want what I want, and that is to punish you and ruin your relationship with Jay, leaving room for me." Suddenly, someone I'd never expected to see came in.

"Valerie! Oh, Valerie! Thank God!" I was so relieved to see a friendly face until she started laughing like the joke was on me. Autumn moved from the bed and joined along too.

"Long time since we came together under these circumstances. Having fun? I guess not, since you're away from Jay, huh. Oh! Wait a minute. You were already away from him, but we knew you couldn't stay away too long since you always seem to run back."

It suddenly clicked that she was the person behind me when we left the hotel. I knew the voice seemed familiar, but I wasn't completely sure.

"Val, what's going on? So... you're not here to help me, are you?" I concluded.

"Fuck no!"

My mouth fell over slightly, accompanied by a feeling of dread and hopelessness

that sat upon me.

"Why, Valerie! What have I ever done to you? I thoug—"

"You thought what?" she yelled. "That I was your friend? You get away with so much shit, it makes no sense. Poor little Shanell," she teased. "Why not let her go on the cruise because her ex-boyfriend scratched her face. I spent a whole fuckin' year listening to your whining after you chose to leave Jay, when you first started at *Lit Mag*. Then the minute you interviewed him, instead of getting closure, your dumb ass—" she said, forcing her finger repeatedly in my temple "—got back with him."

"Why would that even matter to you? I thought you were my friend. I thought I could talk to you and you understood."

"I swear you think the world revolves around you. Jay this! Jay that! It was *me* who called the cops when El had Jay tied up, but what did I get afterwards? Not a thank you, no praise, any type of gratitude would've sufficed." She got back in my face. "You gave me nothing!" She moved and started pacing the floor while she looked toward it. Autumn was being silent the whole time, watching her chastise me and smiling, taking everything in. "You think Jay is so great. He's not! He was all over me in the club."

"When?" Interrupted Autumn.

"Told me how pretty I was, had his arm around me talking in my ear..." She smiled at me. "He didn't want me to tell you any of this, but he obviously didn't know who he was talking to." She came back beside me. "I was your friend until you decided to shit on me for Jay. I was in love with you, *friend*. Did you know that?" I was floored, and she noticed. "Aw, don't act so surprised. Anything you needed, I supplied, which is why you would always come to me. Going for drinks together, having lunch brought to you and inviting me to sit in your office while you ate it—I thought we were connecting until Jay returned."

"But I never gave you any reason to think that I was—"

"Attracted to me? Oh, *sure* you didn't," she toyed. You were sending signals like a coach giving plays. It doesn't matter now, because I've just turned into your worst nightmare. You see, I'm your enemy now, and you're about to find out how much I fuckin' dislike you."

"Valerie, I always, *always* was grateful to you. You have to believe that, and if I ever gave you the wrong impression, I'm so sorry," I wailed.

"Smack!"

She hit me in my face, making my neck swing to the other side of the hit. I swallowed hard. Before, I was fearful when I saw Autumn, but seeing this being done by someone I thought I could trust, really scared me. Nonetheless, I knew I had to get it together for the sake of my little ones, because my heart palpitations were strong, and I didn't want to pass out. I tried to remain as calm as I could in front of them since I didn't want them to get any ideas and hurt me any further or harm my babies. I was hoping and praying that Jay would find a way to find us and soon.

Jay

I was mentally and physically exhausted. Shanell had been missing for a few weeks now. It had turned into a big story, and everyone was on the lookout for her and El. The crazy thing was, they weren't positive that El had something to do with her disappearance. The surveillance video showed two culprits, smaller in stature, that didn't fit El's profile because they were women. They were dressed like nuns, which also made it harder to ID who they were since they were covered, only leaving their eyes exposed. As of right now, they ruled Nikki out as a suspect. She'd been out on Family Medical Leave, and her whereabouts were confirmed, so that raised no concerns or suspicions.

Shanell was eight months now, and I was worried more than ever. I didn't know if she and my babies were okay, if this ordeal had caused her to go into labor... anything! I couldn't sleep and barely wanted to eat, which was really unusual for me. I felt like I was at my lowest. I didn't know where else to look to know where she'd be or where anyone else would've taken her.

My family and friends surrounded me tryna keep my spirits up, but that shit was hard. I still felt alone and empty. I wanted my family, man. Angel being taken away was something I never wanted to relive, and now with Shanell missing, I was sick. I had to figure this shit out.

Her parents were in town tryna help. Her moms couldn't

stop crying, which was understandable. Her dad was tryna be strong, but I could see it was incredibly hard for him too. Nevaeh was going through it. She loved her cousin and missed her, but I noticed my man Marcus was there for her to lean on, even though she still kept her boundaries with him. We all just wanted Shanell and the babies to come home safely and unharmed.

"Nevaeh, won't you sit down?" I told her, since she was pacing the floor on edge. She walked up to me.

"Something just doesn't make any sense to me. El has escaped, but we know he doesn't have Shanell. Shanell was put in a coma by someone giving her morphine. We know that wasn't El, so who gave it to her? El is not the connection. Since Dr. Shaw isn't being charged with malpractice, who the hell drugged her? It damn sure wasn't El, because his ass was locked up, and he wouldn't put no dead black roses on her car and bust out her windshield. As trifling as he is, he don't operate like that. It probably was that crazy ass Nikki. She's the only one that would have access to all kinds of medical supplies and has it in for Shanell. Why the damn police ain't investigating her ass for it?"

When Nevaeh said that, I got to thinking about something else. "Hold on for a second." I thought about Spence finding those syringes in Autumn's medicine cabinet.

Then I thought about Summer telling us their last name was Shaw. I went and grabbed Autumn's journal to see if I could find any missing puzzle pieces since I only looked through it briefly a while ago. The word engaged caught my eyes on one of the pages. I read the sentences surrounding it. *"He actually is engaged! I can't believe it! And then to announce it on the radio making it official! To her! To her? My ass! Oh, what tangled web we weave when I try to be nice, but you deceive...ugh! You think you're ready, but I know that you're not... just wait 'til you get a taste of what I got. You will be all mine!"* I continued looking over more pages. I came across a poem that she wrote. It read: *"The stolen moments we share the shows I never want to miss. Baby your smile is so captivating and your lips I can't wait to kiss. Soon my wait will be over as time is the key, hers would have run out, then you'll be with me."*

It was dated a few days before Shanell's surgery. I felt sick to my stomach. I had been conversing with the enemy all along, and the fact that I slept with her made me more ill. I grabbed a washcloth out of the bathroom and wiped my face off. As I leaned over the sink looking in the mirror, my gut was telling me to check one more thing. I called Shanell's job. Val answered. My tone was even keel, not projecting any emotion either way.

"Hey, Valerie."

"Oh my God! Jay! Have you guys heard anything on Shanell yet?"

"I'm afraid not. I got a question for you? Your cousin Autumn... I just realized her last name is the same as the surgeon that did Shanell's surgery. Are they any relation?"

"Yeah. That's her dad. She works there, unofficially, and helps him out sometimes. Jay, you know my uncle didn't put Shanell in that coma, don't you? I think it was just a bad reaction to the medicine. His record's been clean ever since he's been practice—"

"Okay, thanks for the info. If I hear any news, I'll let y'all know."

It was pretty much official that Autumn was the one that had been behind the threat letters sent to my fan club. I couldn't prove if she was the one who drugged Shanell, but I knew it had to be her. There were police posted outside of my home, so I turned her journal over to them and told them they needed to find Autumn before I did. The officer got one of his colleagues to jump on it right away. I couldn't take sitting around much longer, so I was about to leave to try to find dat ass again myself. Kelli came by the house, stopping me.

"Jay!" Her eyes shifted as she stared at me. I knew I looked rough and scruffy. My hair hadn't been cut, my beard was growing in even more, but my ass was clean, which was all I worried about as far as me. "Jay, I've been back and forth about telling you this, especially at a time like this, but I think you really need to know what you're dealing with."

"Kelli, what is it?" She had a file in her hand that was copied. She showed it to me. It held a few documents in it, one being results of a DNA test performed on Shanell that wasn't requested. I was still tryna figure out what I was looking at and what she was tryna say.

"Get to the point, man. What's this mean?"

"Jay, I believe Nikki requested that a DNA test be done

on Shanell to prove to you that her baby was yours. She just changed the name somehow afterwards."

"Wait! What!" I snapped, shaking my head. "I can't do this right now, Kelli. I can't."

"I know Jay, and I'm sor—"

"But how would Shanell be able to take a DNA test without her even knowing or when that shit happened?"

"Jay, Shanell has been back in forth in the hospital having so many tests done. She probably thought it was routine. Whoever performed it didn't tell her it was a DNA test, because I'm sure she would've questioned it. Nikki must've had it done on her this last time when she was in there." She put her hand on her chin in thought for a second. "She may have been the one to make sure she was back in the hospital this last time, so she could've had it done."

"What you mean?"

"Shanell was dilating prematurely. Why? Because of those pills that she was taking. She was put in the hospital for a couple of days and then placed on strict bed rest. That had to be when Nikki had it done. You didn't get the results until after that, right?"

"Hold the fuck up... Nikki and Shanell don't even have the same DNA, so how's that even possible?"

"Right, but the test is performed to see if the child's DNA matches the father's. It would match because Shanell is really carrying your babies."

"So you telling me she never had a DNA test done on Angel?"

"No, she didn't, but forgive me please, because I did after she passed. It was just so much going on with Shanell that didn't add up, so I conducted my own private investigation because I had my suspicions about Nikki."

"And... what it say?"

"I'm sorry, Jay, but you weren't a match. I have it right here." She showed me more paperwork that proved Angel was not mine. As if I needed any more fuel to my already heated mood. I wanted to kill Nikki. The fact that she had me believe that I was the father and lost a child... I couldn't wrap my head around that shit.

I blamed myself for the loss of our daughter, and to know she never was mine instantly made me sick. I suddenly had to run in the bathroom to throw up. That wound had been opened all over again. I wanted to find her ass too, but right now, my priority was Shanell.

"Kelli, would you have any idea where Nikki could be?"

"All I know is she staying with a relative. I heard Charmaine mention she wanted to get away."

I gave Kelli a kiss on the cheek.

"Thank you, Kelli. I know I've said it like a thousand times, but I mean it. If you ever need anything, don't hesitate to ask. I got you!"

I filled Spence, E, and Marcus in on everything.

"Just a thought," said Spence. "Summer was so eager to rat on Autumn before. Maybe she could tell us where Autumn is. I mean, it's worth a try.

"Which was what I was going to look into before Kelli hit

me with all this new shit. Glad you put that thought back on my mind. I'll call her."

"Summer! It's Jay!"

"Hey! What can I do you for, Jay?"

"You know where ya sister is?"

"No, she wouldn't tell me, and I didn't ask."

"I really needa talk to her. Please, if you hear from her, let me know. Please! It's urgent that I talk to her."

Two days later, Summer hit me up with Autumn's whereabouts. We got on the

road to see her.

Detective

"They're on the road. Not sure where they're headed, but I'll be calling for backup. He might've just stumbled across something we don't know."

Valerie

I didn't realize how big this was going to turn out. I knew the cops were going to look for Shanell, but damn. I didn't expect it to blow up and be this big. The only thing I had going for me as far as not being indicated was that I maintained going to work while Autumn was here to monitor her.

Since Jay trusted me but had it in for Autumn, I knew I could manipulate the circumstances to keep him off my trail pretty much. Plus, I could still play the concerned friend to get information and see if they heard anything on Shanell's whereabouts or not. I just had to figure out what to do for when she delivered.

While Autumn was upstairs with her, I was figuring things out. We were at a cabin that I owned with an upstairs. That's where Shanell was held in one of the rooms. I knew I had to think fast since she would soon need medical attention.

Chapter Fourteen

A FRIENDLY FACE

S *hanell*

Later in the evening, I was lying in the bed with one hand cuffed to it. They ended up using handcuffs since I had to use the bathroom so often, and the tying and untying was getting to be a bit much. Another unsettling fact... I was starting to have contractions. Autumn just so happened to be in the room alone with me. She was so envious of my belly. She hated the fact that I was carrying Jay's baby. I kept squirming around because I was uncomfortable from the contractions.

"Aw, poor baby. You can't take the pain?"

"Autumn," I winced, "I think you should call a doctor... they're... they're happening more frequently."

"No! I'll deliver you first before I call anyone!"

As one contraction subsided, I found myself, shortly after, breathing through another one.

"Autumn, please! I think I might be going into labor!"

"Good! I can't wait to see this precious baby that Jay made."

Minutes later, the pains were starting to subside, but I continued to act like they were still there.

"Autumn, can you go get Val for me please!" She mocked me.

"Autumn, can you go get Val for me please? No! I'm here!" Then she got in my face and poked my left cheek with her finger. I pushed her away with my free hand, but she just got back in my face.

"I don't care what Val said. Once you deliver this baby, I'm going to leave you here to die, so you might want to hold it in as long as you can."

I was terrified, but I was going to protect my babies at all cost. They had no idea I was carrying twins, and I wasn't telling them, but I knew the chances of me holding on any longer were slim. Then Val walked in the room.

"What's going on in here? I heard yelling."

"Oh, I was just telling her that I couldn't come get you because you were busy, and she didn't want to hear it."

She saw that I was rocking from side to side.

"Shanell, are you in pain?"

"Yes! I've been contracting off and on. I really need a doctor."

Val put her hand on her forehead like she was thinking.

"Okay! Okay! I need to make a phone call. I think I can get someone to come here and check you out. Just hold on tight."

She left the room. Twenty minutes later, I heard all this commotion. Throughout it, I heard Jay's voice.

"Jay!" I yelled.

"Shanell!"

I started bawling.

Jay

Surprised to see her, I pushed Val out of the way, knocking her to the floor the moment I heard Shanell's voice. Luckily, she didn't need to do no talking, because I was fully prepared to shoot first and ask questions later, but hearing Shanell saved her. I ran up the steps in search of my baby. I ain't care about no one else. When Shanell saw me, she happily called my name as I made my way over to her. She had handcuffs on one arm, so she couldn't freely hug me with both, but I wrapped her in my arms and crashed my lips so hard against hers. She tried to kiss me back, but she was so emotional she could only cry.

"Jay, the babies," she snapped as she gathered herself. "I've been having contractions. I need to get to the hospital. I'm concerned."

I looked her over and did the one thing that I was happy to still be able to do. Held her belly in my hands and kissed it.

"Other than that, baby, are you okay?"

"I'm fine, but the babies, Jay! I'm scared! We got to get these cuffs off."

The next thing we knew, the police were barging in the room with us.

"We need an ambulance and somebody needa remove these fuckin' cuffs."

"Mr. Murphy, we've already called for an ambulance and I was given the key by one of the perps we had arrested."

"But there were two," Shanell said.

"We have them both."

I looked at Shanell.

"I was told Autumn was here, but I ain't seen her. Would she happen to be one of 'em?"

"Yes sir," said the officer for Shanell.

Shanell was free, and I helped her up. We hugged once more before going down the stairs to get out of this place. The ambulance had arrived and transported us to the hospital. I let the family know that she was found safe and unharmed. They took a statement from her once she was checked out and settled in a room.

The babies were in fetal distress, so they wanted to try a few techniques first to bring them out of it. If that didn't work, Shanell was going to have to get a C-section. We really hoped the techniques worked so she wouldn't have to deliver prematurely. She had to lay on her left side to relieve the pressure of one of the babies laying on a major blood vessel. They also gave her oxygen and extra fluids in her IV to better oxygenate her blood so it could be returned to the babies to get their heart rate back to normal. Ultimately, she stayed in the hospital for three days.

We found out that Autumn was the one that gave Shanell morphine, so she would also be charged with that along with kidnapping, conspiracy, reckless endangerment, and a lot more since we knew, too, she was behind the threats from my fan club. Valerie also was arrested for her role in funneling Autumn Shanell's information so she would know her schedule, along with the kidnapping and that almost hit and run at the airport and would be charged accordingly. The news of her involvement shocked everyone, me included, but it really was hard for Shanell to digest.

Evidence was found that Nikki tampered with the DNA results and Shanell's medicine, so she also was arrested. I felt bad for her, only because I knew losing the baby had changed her, but her dirt finally had caught up to her, and she was now being held accountable. The last person to get locked up was Cashae. They found out she was harboring a fugitive, which was El, but he left before they could grab him, leaving behind evidence of his presence in her home, so he was still on the loose. They assured me they were still on the case though.

Shanell was floored after she learned all the details of everything that everyone had done against her, for my affections and hers. Even though she was glad that I found her, she still wasn't over everything. She was still hurt behind all the shit I did when I lost my memory—well, what she knew about. Some shit I was too ashamed to admit my damn self, and it was no need to. That point in my life where I was a different person was over. I just had to do damage control. I knew she loved me, and I was going to make it my business to continuously apologize for my part in it all.

Shanell

I finally reached my ninth month. I was so grateful that I didn't have my babies prematurely. As they say, I could pop any day now. Even though my pregnancy wasn't one that any first-time mom dreams of with all the drama and stress I had, I knew I was still blessed. With everything that I went through, God still saw to it that I was able to carry my babies full term. What the devils themselves tried to take away from me, God had my back and never left my side.

Jay told me that Nikki lied about the baby and that it wasn't his after all. I felt so bad for him because I knew how much pain that caused him when that baby passed, and to know she never was his—that was beyond words. I never knew how evil spirited some people could be, until the ones that had recently crossed my path.

Jay still thought of Angel as his own, and biologically or not, she would always be his baby girl. El had yet to be caught, I heard. The police were still on the hunt for him. All Jay knew was he better not cross his path. I couldn't worry about El anymore. My focus now was my babies, and if he dared to come near me again or them, I would kill him.

Today, they were throwing a baby shower for me since I was doing so well, and it couldn't get planned earlier. They didn't want to bombard me after my ordeal, so they gave it some time. Since I had yet to pop, they were throwing me one to celebrate. It was being held at the house. The family wanted to keep things as simple as possible, so getting an outside space was out of the question.

Kelli took me to the mall so I could walk around since now they wanted the twins to come, hopefully on their own. When we got back, I was so surprised, mostly to see everyone. Jay's family and some of my co-workers were even here. Both my parents were here; Nevaeh and Lyric were even back.

They both had scores to settle with Nikki, Cashae, Val, and Autumn. Jail wasn't even a good enough punishment for those ladies in no one's eyes. For them, it wasn't over. Even Kelli wanted a piece of the action, but today was about me. Everyone was so happy to see me, still very much pregnant and smiling.

There were so many gifts everywhere, and that was just on the first level. I was told there were even more downstairs. I noticed Jay wasn't around. I figured maybe he didn't want to stick around for all this baby stuff. A few hours later, he came home. By then I was opening my presents downstairs in the rec room. When everyone saw Jay, they were all taunting him saying, "Hi, daddy." He just smiled about it. He walked over and gave me a kiss. Everyone started chanting "Aw." Jay took a chair and pulled it beside me.

"Oh, are you going to open gifts too, daddy?" I teased. He

took the gift I was about to open out of my hand and set it on the floor. Then he motioned his hands for everyone in the room to tone it down because he wanted to speak. I stared at him curiously, wondering what he was up to.

"Y'all don't understand how much I love this woman right here." Different ones in the room responded with words and phrases.

Someone said, "Yes, we do."

Spence coughed up a "Bullshit," and Lyric yelled, "The devil is a liar!" Everyone started laughing at each one of them.

"Nah, but fo'real." He looked at me and smiled. "Shanell, baby, I got some things in store for us." Evan walked over to Jay and gave him a cylinder, and then he gave it to me.

"What's in here?"

"Open it."

I did, and in it contained plans for a new home that Jay was having built for us to move into. I wiped my eyes since the tears were spilling over. I couldn't believe it. It meant so much to me, because I knew how much he loved this house, so to be having one built for us together meant a lot. "Baby, I want us to start fresh. We got the twins coming... I just wanna put all that bad shit behind us." Then he took a ring from his pocket and perched it between his fingers. "I love you with a passion, girl. You know that?" I nodded my head up and down with a tight smile as I set the plans on the floor. "I know I've done some things that's caused you a lot of pain, and you know how bad I wish I could take it back, but we both know I can't. But I said I would spend the rest of my life making it up to you, and I meant that. We were made to be together, right? Baby, would you make me the happiest man alive, and allow me to put this ring back on ya finger and accept being my wife again?"

Without any thought, I stuck my hand out so Jay could put my engagement ring back on, and then we kissed and hugged each other. I noticed afterwards a lot of the ladies in the room were clapping with wet eyes. Jay stayed at the front of the room with me, and we both opened the rest of the gifts. It was a great baby shower, and by the end of it all I was tired.

Once everyone had gone, I needed to have a talk with Jay. I knew I had a lot of healing to do and had to stay prayerful in asking God to make room in my heart for forgiveness. We made it up to the bedroom, and I got comfortable on the bed as Jay sat beside me.

"I know I need to forgive you, but I don't know how to do it yet, but I love you, and because of that, I'm willing to give you another chance. Give *us* another chance, but let me be very clear. By no means am I being your fool. I may love you, but I can leave you alone. I may have agreed to be your wife, but I'm not your wife yet. I have no problem walking out the door if you cheat or be dishonest with me about anything. This right here—" I said, resting my hand on my belly "—is what matters first, before any bullshit. Understood?"

"Understood."

Jay

I noticed Shanell was a lot stronger than before. It

reminded me of when we first met. How confident she was and setting the expectation. I just loved her even more. The babies ended up being delivered before my birthday. Shanell went into labor a day after the shower, and Asaad Jaheem Murphy—weighing five pounds, fourteen ounces—and Syriah Juelle Murphy—six pounds even—were born. Both were twenty inches long with dimples and a head full of straight, black hair.

As I reflected, I was filled with so many emotions. Happy, sad, and indifferent, which was mostly what I had wrote about during this stressful period. I decided to title my upcoming album something that expressed different facets of my life at this time, but I'll keep that under wraps for now. Just know, it'll be all on another album that's coming to you, soon. Until then... Peace!

The End

CPSIA information can be obtained
at www.ICGtesting.com
Printed in the USA
LVHW081803081020
668326LV00015B/1953